Jérôme Schlomoff

About the Author

ALAA AL ASWANY is the internationally best-selling author of *The Yacoubian Building* and *Chicago*. A journalist who writes a controversial opposition column in Egypt, Al Aswany makes his living as a dentist in Cairo.

Friendly Fire

Friendly Fire

STORIES

Alaa Al Aswany

Translated by
Humphrey Davies

HARPER PERENNIAL

NEW YORK • LONDON • TORONTO • SYDNEY • NEW DELHI • AUCKLAND

HARPER ● PERENNIAL

Originally published in Arabic in 2004 under the title *Niran
sadiqa*.

First published in English in 2009 by the American
University in Cairo Press.

HarperCollins books may be purchased for educational,
business, or sales promotional use. For information please
write: Special Markets Department, HarperCollins
Publishers, 10 East 53rd Street, New York, NY 10022.

FIRST U.S. EDITION

Designed by Andrea El-Akshar

Library of Congress Cataloging-in-Publication Data is available upon request.

ISBN 978-0-06-176663-3

09 10 11 12 13 RRD 10 9 8 7 6 5 4 3 2 1

To Abbas Al Aswany,
my father, who taught me

Contents

Preface

1

THE FIRST FILM SHOW IN HISTORY took place in December 1895 in Paris, at the Indian Salon of the Grand Café, on the Rue des Capucins. One year later, the cinema arrived in Egypt. The first film was shown in Alexandria in November 1896 in a hall owned by an Italian named Dello Strologo. This was a unique event in the life of Egyptians and foreigners living in Egypt alike, and the press of the day was filled with enthusiastic commentary on the new invention. Even the extortionate prices charged for tickets did not put people off. Showings lasted about half an hour and were broken up into a number of separate episodes, none exceeding a few minutes in length and consisting for the most part of scenes from domestic life, on the streets, in forests, and at sea. Despite the naiveté of the subjects and the primitive filming techniques, people were enthralled by cinema, paid for their tickets, and hurried into the screening hall, where they sat on chairs in rows waiting for the magic moment when the lights were extinguished, everything went totally black, and the scenes began to appear on the screen. No doubt, the pleasure felt by the first viewers as they watched real life on the screen for the first time was greater by far than our enjoyment today of the art of the cinema, despite which, that exquisite pleasure brought with it at the time a curious problem. The audience, in that state of extreme excitement that would seize them as they followed the film, would often become so engrossed in its events that they would imagine that what they were seeing was indeed real. Thus, if the sea appeared to be rough with high waves, they would feel terrified, and no sooner did a fast-moving train appear on screen, puffing thick smoke, than many would let out cries of genuine panic and rush to exit the hall, fearing that the train would crush them. When these unfortunate events were repeated Dello Strologo instituted a new tradition: he would wait for the audience members in front of the hall and accompany them to the screen. Then, taking it in his fingers, he would say, "This screen is just a piece of cloth, not much different from a bed sheet. The images that you are going to see are reflected on the screen and do not originate within it. In a short while, you are going to see a speeding train. Remember, gentlemen, that this is only an image of a train, and can therefore do you no harm."

When we read of these happenings today, more than a hundred years later, the panic of the audience appears bizarre and laughable. Nevertheless, to this day, some readers of literature continue, most unfortunately, to make the same confusion between imagination and reality, and this is a problem from which I, like many other novelists, have suffered greatly. In my novel *The Yacoubian Building*, I presented two characters, Abaskharon and Malak—two brothers from a poor Coptic background distinguished by their craftiness, eccentricity, and vivacity. In the course, however, of their bitter struggle for survival, they are by no means above lying and stealing. After publishing the novel, I was taken aback to find a Coptic friend of mine telling me reproachfully, "How dare you present such a debased image of the Coptic character?" My response (which he found quite unconvincing) was that I hadn't been presenting the character of the Egyptian Copt in general but that of fictitious characters who happened to be Copts in just the same way that the novel teems with corrupt Muslim characters, from which fact it was quite impossible to infer that all Muslims are corrupt. Likewise, in my novel *Chicago*, I present a character called Shaymaa, a young woman who wears the headscarf, has come from the Egyptian countryside to Chicago to be a student, and whose stay in America has made her rethink her conservative upbringing. Given that she falls in love with a colleague, with whom a physical relationship gradually develops, and that the novel was published in installments in the newspaper *al-Dustur*, I would receive a weekly dose of insults and curses from readers of extreme religious views because, in their opinion, by presenting as a character a young woman who wore the headscarf and had abandoned her principles, I had harmed the image of all Muslim women who wear the headscarf and, consequently, of Islam itself.

I thought long about the question, "What could drive an educated, intelligent reader to consider the behavior of a fictitious character in a work of the imagination an attempt to harm the image of religion or of a section of society?" To be fair, the responsibility for this confusion should not be placed entirely on the shoulders of the reader. On the contrary, it is connected by fine threads to the nature of literature itself, for two reasons. The first of these is that a large part of the pleasure of reading may be attributed to the fact that it gives power to our imaginations. We take pleasure in imagining the events of the novel and its characters in ways that suit ourselves. These imaginings cannot be realized without the intervention of make-believe, meaning that we are incapable of taking pleasure in reading without deluding ourselves, fleetingly, that what we are reading is not made up but has actually happened. (It is because of this make-believe that the lights are turned off in theaters, whether of stage or screen.) It follows that the confusion that occurs in the minds of some between imagination and reality is an indicator of the artist's excellence in the execution of his work, since he has succeeded in making the reader's make-believe seem true, though, in this case, the make-believe is exaggerated and causes him to cease to distinguish between form and reality.

The second reason lies in the fact that literature is an art of life. The novel is a life on paper that resembles our daily lives, but which is more profound, significant, and beautiful. It follows that literature is not an isolated art. On the contrary, its matter is life itself and it intersects with the human sciences such as history, sociology, and ethnology. This intersection is a double-edged sword. On the one hand, it provides the novelist with inexhaustible ammunition for his writing while on the other, negative, side, it drives some to read works of fiction as though they were studies in sociology, which is fundamentally mistaken. The writer of fiction is not a scholar but an artist impacted emotionally by characters from life, who then strives to present these in his works. These characters present us with human truth but do not necessarily represent social truth.

A work of fiction may be of benefit in that it gives us certain indications concerning a given society but it is incapable of presenting its essence, in the scientific meaning of the term. Sociology, with its field-based and theoretical studies, its statistics and its graphs, is capable of presenting the scientific essence of a given society but this is not the role of the novel or the poem. The character of a young, Egyptian, headscarf-wearing woman in a novel may give us an idea about the feelings and problems of some women who wear headscarves but certainly does not represent all the women who wear headscarves in Egypt. Anyone who wants to know the 'truth' about the phenomenon of the headscarf must consult the studies on the topic conducted by sociologists.

Why am I writing this?

Because this confusion between imagination and truth, between the work of fiction and the sociological study, was applied to my novella *The Isam Abd el-Ati Papers*, much in the manner of a curse, and led to its being banned for many long years. How did this come about?

❖ 2 ❖

On my return from my studies in the United States at the end of the 1980s, I decided to dedicate all my efforts to becoming a writer, while at the same time I was obliged to work as a dentist to earn my living. As a result, my life came to be divided into two completely separate parts—the dignified, well-managed life of a respected dentist, and the life of a free man of letters, devoid of all social shackles and pre-existing rules. Each day, after finishing my medical work, I would throw myself into the discovery of life in its most authentic and exciting forms. I would roam strange places and get to know unusual characters, driven by an insatiable curiosity about and genuine need to understand people and learn from them. How many nights I spent in odd, raucous partying with characters who piqued my interest, following which I would be obliged to go by the house to take a shower and drink a quick cup of coffee before taking off again to start, without having slept, my work at the hospital. Day after day, I worked at forming my own group of amazing characters. I made friends with poor people and rich, retired politicians and bankrupt former princes, alcoholics, ex-convicts, fallen women, religious fanatics, con men, thugs, and gang leaders, all the time maintaining a precise and rigorous distance between the worlds of night and day. Sometimes, despite myself, problems would occur: at the end of one night when I had been drinking at a cheap bar downtown, a fierce quarrel erupted between two drunks, one of whom dragged the other out of the bar and began beating him in the street. With some other well-meaning customers, I rushed to break up the fight and bring about the required reconciliation. The whole scene was accompanied, needless to say, by a huge uproar, loud shouting, and slanderous insults. In no time we heard the sound of a window being opened in the building opposite, and a man, obviously aroused from sleep, appeared and started shouting angrily, threatening to call the police if we did not desist immediately from making such a drunken row. When I raised my head to look at him, I recognized him: it was one of my patients at the clinic. Certain he had seen me, I quietly stole away. A few days later I had an appointment to measure him for a set of false teeth. I received him normally. While I was working, he kept peering at me suspiciously. Finally, no longer able to contain himself, he said to me, "Excuse me, doctor. Do you sometimes spend the evenings in places downtown?" I was expecting the question, so I gave him an innocent smile and said in the accents of a professional liar, "I can't go out in the evenings during the week as I have to wake up early to do my surgical procedures, as you know."

The patient gave a sigh of relief and said, "That's what I thought too. Not long ago, I saw someone who looked like you in the street at four in the morning, but I told myself it couldn't possibly be you."

Fortunately, however, such incidents didn't occur often. One night, when on my fascinating nocturnal wanderings, I ran into Triple Mahmoud. A friend had introduced me to him and I had been captivated from the first moment by his extraordinary intelligence and the originality of his ideas. He was different from anybody else I had known. Even his name was unique, his father and grandfather for some reason favoring Mahmoud over any other name, which made his name Mahmoud Mahmoud Mahmoud. This had excited the mockery of his colleagues at school, where they named him Mahmoud Times Three, or Triple Mahmoud, and this name had stuck with him until even he came to use it. When

I met him, Mahmoud was a little over forty and his life could be summed up as a series of determined but unsuccessful attempts to succeed in a variety of fields. At university he had studied—one after the other—engineering, fine arts, and cinema, only to abandon them all. When I asked him the reason, he replied, "I realized that the educational system in Egypt leads to the stifling of creativity in the student, and, in addition, to his being tortured psychologically." When I looked dubious, he added by way of clarification that "the great artists and pioneers of cinema in Egypt created the cinema first, and only established the Institute of Cinema later, proving that they didn't need the institute's classes in order to create the cinema."

This strange and eccentric logic, which was not without its validity, was an example of Mahmoud's take on life, and most of his actions and thoughts were characterized by the same equal mix of eccentricity and original thinking. He was incapable of getting along with stupidity, bureaucracy, and social hypocrisy and was straightforward, frank, and sensitive to the highest degree to any slighting of his opinions or personal dignity—all characteristics designed to bring failure in their wake in the corrupt situation in which we live in Egypt. All the same, despite his rejection of the educational system, he was far from lazy. Once persuaded by an idea, he would exert honest and exceptional efforts to see it put into practice. He was also one of the most diligent readers I have met in my life, having educated himself so well that he had attained an encyclopedic knowledge of art, history, and literature. He was a gifted painter but his first exhibition, in Egypt, failed to attract the interest he had expected, so he decided to take his paintings to France and exhibit them there, telling his friends, "I shall take my art to those who understand art." Someone asked him, "How can you go to France when you don't know a word of French?" Staring at him with contempt, as though calling down curses on his stupidity, he said, "Am I going to France to talk?"

Needless to say, he failed in France, where, as he sat on a sidewalk on the banks of the Seine, he described his situation with a mixture of sarcasm and bitterness as that of "a hungry bankrupt, on whom and on whose paintings the heavy rain descends."

I stayed friends with Mahmoud for a good while, and he had an impact on me. I was fond of him and felt very sad at the way in which his fate had become so circumscribed. A few years later, Mahmoud suffered a nervous breakdown; he was treated in clinics more than once. Then he fell into the slough of narcotics and this led to his early and sudden death at an age of less than fifty. My sorrow over Mahmoud was both personal and general. On the one hand, I sympathized with the trials of one blessed with authentic talent who harbors great hopes only to see them all dashed. On the other, I felt that in all fields Egypt was losing major talents and forces, such as Mahmoud, through tyranny and corruption. Had Mahmoud been born in a democracy, whose citizens had access to justice and nuturing, he would have had a different fate in both art and life. I thought about the tragedy of Mahmoud so much that one day I woke up and asked myself, "Why not write about him? How he would feel and how he would think, and how he would throw out those profound, mocking, intelligent comments that rest on the knife edge between wisdom and madness?" I assumed the character of Mahmoud as though I were an actor, and this was not particularly difficult to do as he had occupied my thoughts so much. The moment I placed a ream of paper in front of me and opened my pen, I set to and I wrote a number of pages at one sitting. I continued working enthusiastically, day after day, until the book was finished. Its protagonist, Isam Abd el-Ati—a frustrated, highly educated young man who suffers from the tyranny, corruption, and hypocrisy in Egyptian society and compares these with the false discourse of self-congratulation repeated by the government media about the greatness of the Egyptians and their millennia-old civilization—bears a close resemblance to Triple Mahmoud.

The novella, which is written in the first person, starts with the hero bitterly mocking the famous words of nationalist leader Mustafa Kamil, "If I weren't Egyptian, I would want to be Egyptian," after which follows a torrent of biting criticism directed at Egyptians. In truth, it never occurred to me while I was writing the book that it would cause me problems. I showed it to friends and all were enthusiastic in their praise and this encouraged me to take the manuscript to the General Egyptian Book Organization (GEBO) with the idea of submitting it for publication and completely confident that it would win their attention, and perhaps even a warm welcome. But there, in the Organization's sumptuous building on the Corniche, Egypt's corrupt cultural establishment dealt me my first shock. It turned out that it was the custom at the GEBO to divide authors into three categories. The first consisted of well-known authors, and these had their works published straightaway. The second consisted of authors who came with a recommendation from someone important in the state, and their works were published too, depending on the degree of influence of the person making the recommendation and without regard for the quality of the work or the author's talent. The third category, which constituted the vast majority of authors, was made up of the obscure ones—authors who were not famous and came without recommendations. These had their works referred to reading committees. The strange thing was that the members of the reading committees were not professors of literature but ordinary employees of the Organization whose bosses had wanted to flatter or reward them and had therefore put them on the committees so that they could earn extra remuneration. In other words, an employee in the Finance Department, or Workers' Affairs, would be the one to decide whether your novel deserved to be published. In fact, the Organization's administration did not pay great attention to the reports of the reading committees, as the authors referred to them were obscurities who had no relationships with the officials. Hence the publication of their works was a matter of no interest to anyone at GEBO.

I will never forget the critical moment when I found myself sitting in front of the employee who constituted the reading committee. He had my book before him on the desk and was flipping through it. Suddenly he said to me, with frowning face and hostile tone, "I can't possibly publish this book."

"Why?"

"Don't tell me you don't know the answer."

"Please tell me yourself."

"Because you insult Egypt."

"I don't insult Egypt."

"You make fun of the leader Mustafa Kamil."

"I don't make fun of him. I love and respect Mustafa Kamil. The one who makes fun of Mustafa Kamil is Isam Abd el-Ati, the hero of the novella."

"Do you want me to believe that you don't agree with what he says even though you're the one who wrote it?"

I started going through for the honorable member of the reading committee the difference between an article and a story, and how the article reflects the author's opinion, while the story is a work of the imagination consisting of multiple characters whose opinions do not necessarily represent the author's point of view.

The employee said nothing. Fired with enthusiasm for my case, I said, "If we follow your logic, the author would be a thief if he writes about thieves and a traitor to his country if he describes the character of a spy in his novel. That kind of logic demolishes the very foundation of literature."

The official manifested a certain embarrassment. Then a crafty smile drew itself on his face and he said, "So you don't agree with the hero's opinion about Egypt?"

"Not at all."

"Are you sure?"

"Of course I'm sure."

"Would you be willing to write a disclaimer?"

"A disclaimer?"

"That's right. I'll agree to publication if you write a disclaimer in your own handwriting condemning what the hero of the book says about Egypt and the Egyptians."

"Very well."

I got a piece of paper and a pen from the employee and wrote as follows, under the heading "Disclaimer": "I, the author of this novella, declare that I do not agree at all with the opinions expressed by the hero, Isam Abd el-Ati. They represent the opposite of what I think about Egypt and the Egyptians." Then I added as my own contribution, "I would like to affirm that the hero of this book is a crazy and mentally unbalanced person and he gets what he deserves at the end. I have written this disclaimer at the request of the reading committee at the General Egyptian Book Organization."

The employee read the disclaimer carefully, sighed with satisfaction, then wrote down the permission to publish on the book and promised me that it would be published soon.

❖ 3 ❖

Why did I agree to write that ludicrous disclaimer? Because I wanted to publish my first book and because I calculated that it would cause a scandal that would reveal the corruption and ignorance at the General Egyptian Book Organization. That was why I added that I was writing the disclaimer at their request. Some weeks passed after this incident and I went once more to the Organization to ask them what was happening with the book. I found a different employee. When I told him what had happened, he took out the book's file (which had not moved from the drawer in the intervening period). As soon as he opened it and read the disclaimer, his face took on an expression of panic. He questioned me and when I told him the story, he said, "No. That's nonsense."

Then he tore up the disclaimer in front of me and told me quietly, "Listen. We will publish this novella once you have taken out the first chapters. What's your reaction?"

My reaction, of course, was to snatch up the manuscript from where it lay on the desk in front of him and leave the building. I have never been back. I was extremely depressed but after a while I pulled myself together and decided to publish the book at my own expense. As I'd completed a collection of short stories during the same period, I put the stories and the novella together in one book, printed just three hundred copies, and distributed these to critics and friends. The book met with an astonishingly warm welcome and was praised by many critics. This put me in a strange situation for a period—that of being a writer without readers. The critics praised my book in the newspapers, but anyone who read those articles and then went looking for the book would not be able to find it. Bad luck, in fact, continued to dog the work. After the great success of *The Yacoubian Building*, publishers started pressuring me to give them anything I'd written. I took *The Isam Abd el-Ati Papers* to a major publisher, who read it and said, "I like it very much, but frankly I can't take on the consequences of publishing it. The opinions expressed in it could get me put in jail." Indeed, a well-known critic, who hates me for personal reasons, wrote, without the slightest embarrassment or sense of guilt, a long article in which he deliberately confused me with the hero of the story, using this confusion as a base from which to accuse me of despising my country and of being infatuated with the West.

This is the history of the book that you are holding in your hands, which I wanted you to know before you start reading it. I am confident that the majority of readers will understand that literary characters always possess an existence independent of the writer. As for those who would hold me to account for the opinions of the hero and consider me responsible for them, I repeat to them, with respect, what Dello Strologo, the owner of the Italian cinema said one day to his audience: "This screen is just a piece of cloth, on which images are reflected. In a short while, you are going to see a speeding train . . . . Remember, gentlemen, that this is only an image of a train, and can therefore do you no harm."

Friendly Fire

The Isam Abd el-Ati Papers

❖ 1 ❖

If I weren't Egyptian, I would want to be Egyptian.

—Mustafa Kamil*

I HAVE CHOSEN THIS SAYING as the first words of these papers of mine because they are, in my opinion, the dumbest thing I've ever heard. They represent (assuming that the one who said them really meant them) the sort of stupid tribal loyalty that makes my blood boil every time I think of it. What if the good Mustafa Kamil had been born Chinese, for example, or Indian? Would he not have repeated the same phrase out of pride in his Chinese or Indian nationality? And can such pride have any value if it's the outcome of coincidence? And if Mustafa Kamil could choose—of his own conscious volition,

---

* *Mustafa Kamil (1874–1908) was an Egyptian nationalist leader.*

as he would have us believe—to be Egyptian, there would have to be important reasons to make him so choose. He would have to find in the Egyptian people some virtues not to be found in any other. What, then, might such virtues be? Are the Egyptians distinguished by, for example, their seriousness and love of work, like the Germans or the Japanese? Do they love risk-taking and change, like the Americans? Do they honor history and the arts, like the French and the Italians? They have no such distinguishing characteristics. What then does distinguish the Egyptians? What are their virtues? I challenge anyone to cite me a single Egyptian virtue. Cowardice and hypocrisy, underhandedness and cunning, laziness and spite—these are our characteristics as Egyptians. And because we know the truth about ourselves, we cover it over with a lot of shouting and lies—empty, ringing slogans that we repeat day in day out about our 'great' Egyptian people. And the sad thing is that we've repeated these lies so often we've ended up believing them. Indeed—and this is truly amazing—we've arranged these lies about ourselves as songs and anthems. Have you heard of any other people in the world doing such a thing? Do the English, for example, sing, *Ah England, O Land of Ours! Your earth is of marble made, your dust with musk and amber laid*? Such banalities are an integral part of our make-up. Imagine, in the reader set for Second Year Elementary, I read the following words: "God loves Egypt very much and talked about her in His Noble Book. This is why He has blessed her with our lovely clement climate, summer and winter, and why He protects her from the wiles of her enemies."

See the tissue of lies that they stuff into children's heads? That "lovely clement climate" of ours is in fact hell. Seven months from March to October the searing heat roasts our skins until the beasts expire and the asphalt on the streets melts under the blazing sole of the sun—and still we thank God for our beautiful climate! And again, if God protects Egypt from the wiles of her enemies, as they claim, how come we've been occupied by every people on Earth? The history of Egypt is in reality nothing but a continuous series of defeats inflicted upon us by all the nations of the world, starting with the Romans and going all the way to the Jews.

All these stupidities get on my nerves, and what annoys me even more is that we—we pitiful Egyptians—like to bathe in the reflected glory of the pharaohs. Under the pharaohs, the Egyptians formed a truly great nation, but what have we to do with them? We are the corrupt, indeterminate outcome of the miscegenation of the conquerors' troops with their captives from the defeated population. The Egyptian peasant whose land was violated and manhood dishonored at the hands of the conquerors for centuries on end lost everything that linked him to his great ancestors, and from his long acquaintance with humiliation he came to feel at ease with it, surrendered to it, and over time acquired the mentality of a servant. Try to recall the few truly courageous Egyptians you have met in your life. The Egyptian, no matter how high he has risen or how well educated he has become, will cringe before you if you are the stronger, smiling to your face and buttering you up while he hates you and tries to bring about your downfall by some foolproof covert means that will cost him neither confrontation nor danger. A mere servant, that's your Egyptian. I hate the Egyptians and I hate Egypt. I hate it with all my heart and hope it gets even worse and more wretched. Even though I take care to hide this hatred (to avoid stupid problems), sometimes I can't keep it in. Once, at the house of one of my colleagues, I was watching a soccer match between Egypt and an African country called Zaire, and when the African player scored the winning goal, I yelled out loud with joy while the others expressed their disapproval at my happiness at our defeat. I paid them no attention, though, and continued watching, with schadenfreude, the faces of the defeated Egyptians. Their expressions were flat and broken and their features exuded sorrow and impotence. This is the way the Egyptians have really looked for thousands of years.

2

My mind was freed of delusions at one go, a fact of which I am proud, for I have known many men, some of them intelligent and well educated, who wasted their lives on phantasms—beliefs and theories the dupes spent years chasing like a mirage. Nationalism, religion, Marxism—all those dazzling words revealed their spuriousness to me at an early age. Getting rid of religion was easy. Marxism lasted longer. I acknowledge that Marxism has a rational side that deserves respect, and at the same time it leaves a mark on the soul that outlasts the idea itself. I remained a committed Marxist for two years, but I always felt I'd change. I couldn't understand why I should make sacrifices for vulgar creatures like workers and peasants. I used to observe the common people exchanging their banal jokes. I'd watch them on their feast days when they surged onto the streets like over-excited beasts, treading everything beautiful under their blind heavy feet, and Marx's grand words about them would shrivel before my contempt and hatred. Was I going to struggle and die for the likes of those? They were animals who deserved nothing but derision and to be ruled by terror; that was the only language they understood. Try just once for yourself being weak in front of one of them and see what he does to you.

With the passing of Marxism, I achieved full control over my mind and its liberation, and then I felt lonely. Delusions, much as they deceive you, also keep you company. The cold severe truth on the other hand casts you into a cruel wilderness. My success in taming my mind was directly paralleled by my failure to gain mastery over my feelings. The most complex mental problems pose no challenge to my thinking but any spontaneous simple interaction with people throws me into confusion and renders me powerless. There is a confirmed inverse relationship between awareness and action by which the people most apt to act are the most lethargic mentally and the dumbest, and vice versa. As awareness grows, so the ability to act is disturbed. My head—which never stops thinking and reviewing every single possibility and probability—this same head impedes my correct conduct in situations that most people consider quite ordinary and which they negotiate with complete ease. Before I go to visit a friend at his house for the first time, I am kept awake by the thought that the door-keeper, whom I don't know, will stop me and ask me which apartment I'm going to. Worrying over the doorkeeper's question becomes such an obsession for me that I often insist to my friends that we meet in a public place rather than in their homes (without, of course, disclosing the reason to them), and when I'm forced in the end to face the moment when I have to cross the lobby of an apartment block in which my friend lives, I'm as ill at ease as a child, and I whistle, or look at the watch on my wrist, or fiddle with my shirt sleeve, to show that I am not concerned. On such occasions, the doorkeeper's call quickly reaches me, for I will have passed him by, ignoring his enquiry and hurrying on without paying him any attention; but he will rush after me, catch up with me, and finally stop and question me; and, despite that fact that I am expecting the question, I feel each time an immense sense of affront at everything that has happened. When I respond, I sometimes do so roughly and harshly and at other times I am totally demolished before him, stammering and producing my words falteringly and agitatedly; and then the doorkeeper draws himself to his full height, his voice rises, and he stares in my face with wide-open, powerful eyes, for he has sensed my weakness. What I am never capable of in such circumstances is to give the impression of being a self-confident gentleman sure of his capabilities, of answering the doorkeeper in a calm voice and with a smile, and saying, "I'm going to see So-and-so Bey." If I were to answer such a person just once in this fashion, he would back off immediately and be reduced right away to his natural size. This is the poise that I lack and I am incapable of determining if my unbalanced feelings are attributable to my overly developed awareness or to the circumstances of my upbringing. My memories of boyhood and adolescence are imprinted on my mind in a somewhat 'historical' way. When I review the events of my life, I feel as though I were a tragic hero accepting the blows of fate with a noble, courageous heart. Heroes, unlike common people, do not meet with ephemeral, ordinary events: everything that

happens to them is, of necessity, significant and fateful.
Similarly, events are not imprinted on my memory as separate,
scattered flashes but as a continuous line of points that are
joined in a way that can neither be predicted nor prepared for.
I imagine it as being in the form of a cardboard box divided
up by partitions into small, intersecting passageways.

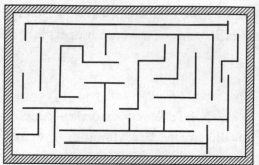

Fig. 2

Fig. 1

   This is what the box looks like from
above (fig. 1). A small wooden doll whose
movements are controlled by numerous
strings (fig. 2) passes through the laby-
rinthine passageways of the box; the
strings are so thin they can barely be
seen, but they are too strong to be cut and
they are gathered in a single large hand,
outside the box. This hand controls the
doll's movements and the owner of the hand sees the box in
its entirety, with all its passageways and turns. The doll, on the
other hand, can see only the passage that it is going down
and the moment it reaches the end of that passage the strings

draw it toward a new one. I am that doll, the cardboard box is my life, and the big hand is the hand of fate.

Fate holds our destinies just as the large hand holds the doll—with implacable, inescapable control. It plays with our capabilities and our wishes and it plays with us, and its sole motive for doing so is its excessive love of play—not goodness or justice or truth or any of that stuff—and if it ever were to grasp the sorrows that it causes us, were ever to feel the pain that it inflicts on us, it would hide its face in shame at its doings.

❖ 3 ❖

Ever since he was a child, he'd loved to draw—people's faces, trees, the cars in the streets. Everything his eyes saw was imprinted in detail on his young mind. Then the lines he made would run over the paper to re-shape things into the way he wanted to see them. When he reached fifteen, his love of drawing became a problem because he neglected his schoolwork altogether. Every morning, he'd escape from the school and use his pocket money to buy coloring pencils and a sketchbook. Then he'd go to the municipal garden in Zaqaziq, isolate himself on an empty seat, and draw.* His father dealt with him harshly, often beat him, and often hid his pencils from him and tore up his drawings, but none of it was any use: his love of drawing was stronger. When he was twenty, his father died suddenly and that day his fate was decided. The last barrier was broken and he had soon left Zaqaziq, where he had been born, to live in a small room on

---

* *Zaqaziq is a city in the Nile Delta, the capital of Sharqiya Governorate.*

the roof of an old house in the Bein el-Sarayat neighborhood of Cairo. Before two years had passed, he was drawing the main cartoon for three weekly magazines, and at age twenty-four he put on his first exhibition of oil paintings.

These beginnings were worthy, no doubt, of Ragheb, Bikar, or any other great painter, but I'm not talking about any of them.* These were the beginnings of Abd el-Ati, and who has heard of him? Abd el-Ati was my father, and, despite the exciting, promise-packed start, he ended up far from what was expected. Abd el-Ati did not shine and his great hopes as a painter were never realized. He changed nothing in the development of painting, as he had dreamed of doing, and thirty years after his move to Cairo, my father was still an obscure artist earning his living doing drawings for a magazine called *Life* that nobody read and getting by on other small jobs, such as supervising the wall newspapers produced at certain schools and giving private art lessons to the children of the rich. This was where Abd el-Ati was at fifty, and I ask myself, why did my father fail? Was he lacking in talent? For sure he had more than many painters who succeeded and became famous. Was it laziness and love of pleasure that did for him? On the contrary, my father spent money on alcohol and drugs only during his last years. Before then, he used to produce prolifically and persistently and when I was little I'd often wake in the morning to find he hadn't slept but spent the entire night on a new painting. I loved him then. His eyes would be exhausted, his

---

* *Sabri Ragheb (1920–2000) and Hussein Bikar (1912–2002) were both well-known Egyptian painters.*

face drawn, and his laugh low and satisfied. He'd dry his hands quickly on his paint-spattered smock and bend down to kiss me and his good, coarse smell would take possession of me. Then he'd take me by the hand, pull me back a little, point to the painting on its easel, and ask me, pretending to be very grave, "What think you, my dear sir, of the work? Do you like it?"

My mother would protest laughingly and say, "You're asking Isam? What can the child know about painting?"

And my father would reply, picking me up in his arms and kissing me, "What do you mean? He will be a great artist. One day I'll tell you, 'I told you so!'"

❖

If it wasn't laziness or lack of talent, then what was it? When I got older, I worked out the reason. What my father lacked was charisma—that halo that encircles great men and grants them influence over others.

Charisma is not a quality that can be acquired but is given to some and not others. Those who have it are born with a place reserved for them at the top. All they have to do for admiration and appreciation to be showered upon them is to work with a certain proficiency. The efforts of those who don't have it are a hopeless battle against nature that they are fated to lose, and no matter how much such people may wear themselves out over their work, the appreciation of others will come to them hesitantly, permeated with doubt and reserve.

The person who discovered the New World wasn't Christopher Columbus but an aged sailor called Pinzón who was his shipmate. Pinzón pointed out the right route to his captain and then his name fell into oblivion under the impact of the clamor of glory that erupted around the name of the immortal, charismatic Columbus.

My father's fate was Pinzón's—to be created without luster, as ordinary as millions of others like him who have nothing to distinguish them. Of medium build, bald, and a little fat. You could sit with him for a whole hour, then he'd leave and you wouldn't give him a second thought, and you'd probably get his name wrong if you met him again. His voice had a slight huskiness to it which people listening to him would assume was about to disappear, leaving a clear sound that would hold the attention of those who heard it. But the huskiness would not disappear and my father's voice would emerge as though constricted, the words running into one another. He spoke fast, the words tumbling out of his mouth, and he was incapable of holding people's interest if he spoke anything more than short phrases. If this happened people would turn their attention to other speakers, at which point my father would tug on their sleeves or grip their shoulders with his fingers to keep their interest, looking at such moments like a helpless child whose mother is getting ahead of him in the crowd, so that he has to cling onto her skirts in order not to get lost. At home, my father wasn't one of those husbands who lay down the law; rather, he obeyed my mother in everything. I never felt any awe of him when I was young and sometimes when he scolded me a malign and delicious urge would push me to challenge his authority. When I reached the secondary school, my friends at the Ibrahimiya School were astonished when I told them that my father knew that I would play truant. I used to calmly tell my father that I wasn't going to school the next day but was going to the movies, and he would listen to me and then fiddle with his mustache—a habit of his when agitated or surprised— then pretend for a moment to be thinking, and ask me with a sort of irritated laugh that passed for permission, "Aren't you afraid you'll miss something important if you play hooky?"

And that would be it—a question, and the matter left to me. If I ignored the question, things ended there. If, however, I hesitated and seemed to be thinking it over, he'd be encouraged and would rush to talk to me enthusiastically about the importance for regular study. Then he'd say, in an uncertain voice, "I don't know, you know. I don't think there's any call for this playing hooky thing. What do you think?"

My father was weak and as a result his life ended in total defeat. But despite his failure and his weakness, I liked him. I liked him because he accepted his defeat with the silence of one who knows the rules. He didn't fill the world with lament and he didn't turn into a poisonous insect. On the occasion of a major competition, my father would await the result among the other competitors, and, when he found out that he'd lost and someone else had won, he wouldn't express astonishment or anger but carefully gather his things together, smiling sadly, and then make haste to catch the last bus and, if he felt comfortable with the passenger sitting next to him, would tell him everything that had happened, in a neutral tone of voice. His neighbor would listen to him, at first with pity, but then some small thing—such as my father's shoes or his shirt or even an expression that passed over his face—would cause him to understand why he had failed and the man would feel less, or even not at all, sorry.

❖

Lots of people spent their evenings at our house. There were many names belonging to people of differing professions and ages. As some disappeared through travel, or death, new faces appeared. Despite their differences, they were joined by a common thread: all were major unfinished works. El-Ghamdi was a teacher of Arabic language who had once hoped to be a poet. Muhammad Irfan was a former Marxist who had abandoned his dream of changing the world and made do with arts journalism; he made up news items about dancers and singers and blackmailed them. Even 'Uncle' Anwar I discovered from my father, had dreamed of being a great songwriter and had ended up playing backing zither to the dancer called Sugar. And there were many others. A band of people with shattered dreams, like old people carping at a wedding, who met every evening to curse blind luck and the lousy times: "We knew So-and-so when he used to pray God for the price of a cigarette, and now he's got more money than he knows what to do with, with a villa in el-Maadi, a chalet in cl-Agami, and three luxury cars. And So-and-so, the famous singer—didn't he fail the radio test in the fifties? You can believe that story because I was a member of the committee!" When I sat with my father's friends, I never felt for an instant that they loved one another. They feuded all the time and violent quarrels were always breaking out among them. Nevertheless, they took care to come and never broke with one another because what joined them was stronger than their enmity. They needed these gatherings, because at them their sense of inadequacy was dissolved in their awareness of their common fate, and when they met none of them was embarrassed by his failure.

I would use any excuse to escape from sitting with them and only stay up late with them if Uncle Anwar was present. Uncle Anwar was different. He was my father's closest friend, the two of them joined by thirty years of friendship. Once they had lived together in a single room on Bein el-Sarayat, my father dreaming of painting, Anwar of music. Anwar earned a lot from his work with Sugar and spent lavishly on himself and his friends. He had never married because marriage, in his opinion, gave you the blues and the blues shortened your life. Uncle Anwar was nice. He never stopped making fun of things and stirring those around him to laughter. On what he called 'nights of joy,' which were those following the wedding of some rich person, Uncle Anwar would appear in the circle bearing 'goodies'—a big bottle of brandy, an ounce of good-quality hashish, and a kilo of kebab and sweetbreads, and when his friends received him with cheers, Uncle Anwar would affect a grave face, throw down in front of them the things that he had brought, and pronounce, in the tones of a strict father, "Eat and drink until a white thread can be distinguished against the black hides of your miserable fathers!"*

Uncle Anwar hated nobody so much as he hated Sugar, the dancer, against whom he directed the greater part of his jokes and calumniations. Sometimes, even, when conversation had dried up and silence reigned, one of those present would ask Anwar for news of his mistress and Anwar would launch into a virtuoso display of sarcasm at the expense of Sugar's ignorance, arrogance, rich lovers, and general awfulness, and the

---

* In Ramadan, Muslims are required to start fasting from the time just before dawn when a white thread can be distinguished from a black thread. The words reference the Qur'an 2:187.

place would ring with laughter once more. Despite Anwar's imperious love of music, he would go whole nights without playing, refusing immediately and roughly if anyone asked him to do so, and if anyone insisted, a fight would sometimes break out. Anwar's friends knew how he was and so didn't ask him, knowing that, at a given moment, which no one could predict, Anwar would suddenly stretch out his hand, take the zither, put on the plectra, and start to play. If one contemplated his face after a few minutes of playing, it would seem that he could no longer see the audience or make out his surroundings. When Anwar finished, he would receive the shouts of admiration and the applause with a face drawn and pale and he'd remain like that for a while before resuming his unruliness and sarcasm, at which point we'd know that he'd returned.

❖

There are no weddings on Tuesdays. Uncle Anwar would show up early, the first to arrive, his face still bearing the traces of sleep and battered by the din of the previous night's show. He would greet my mother politely and make his way to the studio. There, he would remove his suit, hang it up carefully, and put on his gallabiya (Uncle Anwar always kept one of his gallabiyas at our house). After a little while my father would come. They would drink tea together and then sit on the floor and busy themselves preparing the equipment for the evening. They began with the goza, or hand-held waterpipe, the cleaning and readying of which were important tasks that kept both Anwar and my father busy and often gave rise to arguments. My father might be of the opinion that it was the pieces of thick paper used to tighten the joints that were impeding the flow of the smoke, while Anwar might claim that it was the reed stem that was blocked. I used to watch them—Anwar in his striped gallabiya, seated cross-legged and tearing up little pieces of paper that he would stuff between the stem of the waterpipe and the tobacco bowl and my father next to him, repeatedly puffing into the mouthpiece of the reed and listening to how the water gurgled. When they came to Cairo thirty years before, two young artists full of determination and ambition, had it ever occurred to them that things would turn out like this? How distant the beginning seemed now and how strange the end! Usually it was Anwar who was the cleverer at diagnosing the goza's problems and when he'd finished placing the tightening wads, he'd light a bowl of tobacco to test it and draw a long breath, which would be followed by a fierce fit of coughing that turned his eyes red. Then he'd pass the pipe over to my father, saying, "I told you it was the wads. They're dandy now. Take a drag and ask the Lord to bless me," and my father would look in my direction and say laughingly, before thrusting the mouthpiece into his mouth, "Your Uncle Anwar, see, before the music, used to work as a goza mechanic on Bein el-Sarayat," and Anwar would burst out with, "Don't say such things, you son of a bitch! You want Isam to get funny ideas about me?"* Then he'd turn to me, an injured expression on his face, and say, "Don't you believe a word your father says, Master Isam! I've been an honest man all my life. It was your father who taught me to smoke hashish and at the beginning I thought it was chocolate."

---

* *Bein el-Sarayat is the name of a street and district in Giza, near Cairo University.*

A hail of jokes and quips would then be released, after which Anwar's face would suddenly resume its serious expression and he'd stand up and thrust his hand into the pocket of his jacket where it hung on the wall and take out a piece of hashish wrapped in cellophane and hand it to my father who would sniff it, try it with his teeth, squeeze it between his fingers, and proclaim it to be, "Sweet, Anwar! Mustafa's? What do you say? Should we wait for the rest or start with a solo?"

Anwar would sit down cross-legged again and say in tones of the utmost seriousness, "Let's start with a solo in the mode *Sika*."*

He would bite the hashish into little pieces which he would distribute among the pipe bowls of molasses-soaked tobacco, then light the charcoal, and set to smoking right away. They'd ask me to stay with them and I'd sit and smoke with them, and after a few pipes the drug would go to Anwar's head, his puffy eyelids would droop, a grave expression would appear in his eyes, and he'd nod his head as though following an inner dialogue that none but he could hear. Then he'd turn to my father, smile, pat him on his thick leg, and say, "Honestly, my dear Mr. Abduh, don't you think you should have given up all this painting business? You could have learned to be a belly dancer. What's wrong with belly dancing? By now you'd be something of a different order entirely. Old Woman Sugar does *this* (here Anwar would twitch his waist, holding his arms up as though dancing) and gets five hundred pounds a night, the bitch."

---

* Sika *is a mode in Arabic music beginning on E half flat and having B half flat.*

17

My father would be on the verge of responding when Uncle Anwar, all taken with zeal, would suddenly leap up, halfway through the pipe, and cry, "What do you say, Abduh? It's really too bad of you! I'm telling you, all you have to do is *this* and you get five hundred pounds," and Anwar and my father would dissolve into a long bout of laughter.

At lunch my father would drink a glass of rum, a habit that helped him to sleep well during his siesta, or so he said. The rum would send its warmth through my father's body and he'd talk to us—me and my mother—and laugh, and sometimes a mysterious melancholy would seep into him, but on this one day he seemed more than usually upset. He kept fiddling with his mustache in silence, his eyes staring into space, and when my mother asked him, "What's wrong with you?" my father (who seemed to have been waiting for the question) sighed deeply, took a gulp from his glass of rum, and said, playing with a matchstick between his teeth, "Would you believe, I got a letter today from someone who admires my work."

My father seemed embarrassed and went on in a louder voice as though saying something he'd prepared ahead of time, "Naturally, I'm happy, as any artist would be, to get a letter from an admirer. But what makes me happier is that there's someone out there who actually follows the figurative arts in Egypt in these days of ours."

There was silence for a moment and my father took a sip from his glass. I looked at my mother and got the impression that she wanted to say something but hadn't yet worked out what, so I jumped in with, "So where's the letter?"

"Over there by you, in the pocket of my jacket."

I got up and inserted my hand into the pocket of the jacket hanging on the coat rack in the corner of the parlor, and pulled out the letter. The envelope was written in an elegant black hand "Abd el-Ati, *Life*, 6 Qasr el-Aini Street." I opened the envelope and pulled out the letter, and as I started reading my mother exclaimed, "Read it out loud, Isam."

I haven't mentioned the sender's name, which was Mahmoud Ali Farghal, from Minyet el-Nasr, Governorate of el-Daqahliya. He said that he worked as a school art teacher and did oil paintings and dreamed of becoming a great artist like my father. He asserted that he followed my father's work in *Life* every Wednesday and had seen one exhibition that my father had put on in Cairo some years ago and that though he'd come to Cairo especially to see the exhibition, and had wanted to talk with my father, his great shyness had prevented him from introducing himself. All the same, he averred again that he would be visiting my father soon at his *Life* office so as to make his acquaintance and show him his work. He ended the letter with the words, "Kindly accept the salutations of your pupil and disciple, Mahmoud Ali Farghal."

That Farghal was a genuine admirer of my father's work was a possibility not to be dismissed, for one is always coming across a certain type of person who interests himself in matters no one but he knows anything about and gets very enthusiastic about them, such as the people who support the Tirsana soccer club or devotees of the voice of Abd el-Latif el-Tilbani, for example.* Equally possible was that Farghal

---

* *Tirsana is a soccer club in the lower echelons of the Egyptian soccer league; Abdel Latif el-Tilbany was a singer with a small following.*

was a hypocrite who wanted to get close to my father so that the latter could help him in some way or give him an introduction to someone.

When I finished reading the letter, my father was blushing with ecstatic joy. He started fiddling with the fork on his empty plate, a happy look in his eyes, and he pursed his lips like a child trying not to smile. My mother, who only now seemed to have taken in what was happening, burst out with, "Wonderful, Abduh! Congratulations! I think we ought to frame the letter and hang it in the sitting room."

I laughed out loud and my father shouted in protest, "What's all this nonsense about framing and hanging? You really are a dumb cow."

My mother turned pale for a moment but then burst out laughing and mumbled, "Never mind, never mind. No framing. Don't get mad."

My father lit a cigarette and explained to her, this time in a calm, restrained voice, that his happiness was not because he had an admirer but on behalf of the figurative arts, an idea that he then expatiated on at length and in various formulations. Then he moved on to a lot of stuff about the great artist's duty toward the talent of the rising generation and spoke about his professors of painting and how they'd encouraged him. I felt that my father was looking forward to the day when he would meet Farghal and that he would make every effort to help him.

My father went into his room to sleep, my mother took the dishes into the kitchen, and I sat on my own. The letter still lay before me on the table. I looked at it. Farghal's writing was beautiful and polished. I stretched out my hand and took the letter and the feel of the paper on my fingers was smooth and uniform. I looked at the picture of my father and mother in their wedding clothes that hung on the wall. At first I thought about the style of my father's suit in the picture. Then I lost my concentration for a moment and found myself grasping the piece of the paper in my hands. I was tearing it in half. The tearing made a quietly rough sound. An obscure anxiety gnawed at me when I finished but I dismissed it and hurried—as though to reassure myself—to rip it into small pieces, and then even smaller ones. Each time it got harder to tear the paper but I continued until the paper had been turned into little bits, scattered everywhere, which I gathered carefully in my hand. I then went into the kitchen and threw these out of the window that gave onto the light shaft in the center of the building and watched the breeze scatter them everywhere. Afterward, I exchanged a few ordinary words with my mother, left her, went to my room, and slept.

That evening, my mother woke me up and said, as she offered me a glass of tea, "You father wants to see you." I wasn't thinking about anything specific and said to myself I'd drink my tea, smoke a cigarette, and then wash my face and go see him.

The evening session was in full swing as usual and I was greeted by a thick cloud of smoke and the piercing smell of hashish. My father's bloodshot eyes showed me that he'd been smoking for a while. Uncle Anwar sang out his welcome.

"Hello, Isam! Where've you been?"

My father invited me to sit down, so I sat, and Uncle Anwar held out the goza to me, but I declined because I had to study, to which Uncle Anwar responded, as he put the mouthpiece into his mouth, "What of it? Is that any reason not to? You can do your best studying when you're stoned. Did you know that when I was in Secondary I'd roll my usual couple of cigarettes, settle back, and then the biggest bitch of a math problem wouldn't take me a second?"

"Which would explain why you made such a mess of school, you loser!"

So cried Muhammad Irfan before bursting into laughter, and other low laughs issued from those present. I sensed that the atmosphere was strained for some reason and it wasn't long before I realized that my entrance had interrupted a heated discussion between my father and el-Ghamdi.

El-Ghamdi was over fifty but seemed younger. He was good-looking, with wide green eyes and well-defined strong clear features. His chestnut hair was combed carefully back and he had a light rosy complexion. I found something off-putting about the man, the same thing I often find in Arabic language teachers—a meekness of spirit and a hateful clinging nature. El-Ghamdi smiled and said in a clear voice and measured tones, as though he were a professor delivering the lesson of the day to his students, "Your problem, Abduh, is that you're an optimist. Too much so. You have to be aware that art and literature in Egypt are completely dead. We need at least half a century before the Egyptians can recover their interest in the arts, before a real public for the arts can be formed—with all due respect to the colleague who sent you the letter."

He smiled as he spoke and stared with his trusting green eyes into the faces of those around him. It was clear that he was having an effect on them and that they were convinced by what he was saying. My father seemed agitated and bursting to express his disagreement. He squirmed in his seat and sighed. Then he said, his words rapid and staccato, "All the same, Ghamdi, you have to make allowances. A few individuals are enough to make a start."

El-Ghamdi cried out in tones of histrionic disagreement and it became clear that he was determined to carry my father's defeat to the bitter end.

"What start, my dear sir? Wake up! All this fuss because one admirer wrote you a letter, and you want to convince us that there's a public for art in Egypt? Go down into the street and then you'll get it! Make a tour of the bus stops! Look at the people's faces! You think those people could give a damn about art? Those people? When people like that go to sleep all they dream about is finding chickens at the co-op!"

El-Ghamdi laughed and so did everyone else. I didn't, though, and nor did Uncle Anwar, who busied himself cleaning the goza, though he did seem to be following the conversation with interest. El-Ghamdi bent forward where he was sitting and said with the air of one putting an end to the discussion of a trivial subject that has gone on too long, "Listen, Abduh. Let me set your mind at rest. What did you tell me the writer does for a living?"

"He's a teacher," mumbled my father in a low voice.

"I know, but what does he teach?"

My father said nothing for a moment and then he answered, "An art teacher, but . . . ."

"But what? An art teacher and he's not supposed to understand art? At least he'd have the basics that he studied.

An art teacher, who interests himself in the progress of art? My dear fellow, that's you! And you think that that's a sign of artistic awareness? Give me a break!"

El-Ghamdi made a dismissive gesture with his hand, laughed, and looked at the others, like a chess champion who makes a final masterful move that brings the match to an end in his favor. Then he turned back to my father and said in dismissive tones oozing sarcasm, "My dear Professor Abd el-Ati, you're giving this business of the letter more importance than it deserves."

My father cried out to interrupt him, appearing for the first time to be starting to doubt his own opinion, "No! It's got nothing to do with his being an art teacher! I sensed from what he said that he's someone who understands."

"Understands? Someone like that understands?"

El-Ghamdi posed these questions and let out a sarcastic laugh, the malign intent of his words clear to all, since how could anyone who liked Abd el-Ati's work understand anything. My father's face clouded with real anger and he muttered fervently, "Yes, Ghamdi, he understands. I'm certain he understands."

My father looked around him as though he was searching for something. Then he saw me and said, "Isam, go get the letter from inside."

I looked at him and found myself rising slowly and turning toward the door. Perhaps interpreting my hesitation as due to forgetfulness, he said, "You'll find the letter in the parlor. On the table, as I remember."

I turned back once more, looked at my father, and said in hollow tones, "I tore it up."

"What?" shouted my father, his eyes dilating. I felt I was sliding toward the end, so I said, deliberately and slowly, "I tore the letter up."

It was more than he could take. He leaped up and came toward me. He came so close that I could feel the heat of his panting breath on my face. I was expecting him to slap me but he suddenly turned around and shouted, "You're insane! Totally insane! You tore up the letter, you madman?"

He seemed to have nothing more to say, and he started moving, turning, and shouting out the same words, while Uncle Anwar went to him and took hold of him to calm him down and I stood and watched what was happening. I didn't feel fear or regret. My consciousness had been disconnected. I could see my father and Anwar and the people sitting there and they looked to me like undefined, floating shapes. When I came to, I heard my father saying, "Do you hear what I say? Get out of my sight, God damn you!"

Silence reigned for a moment and I heard Uncle Anwar whisper to my father, "That's not the way, Abduh. You're making too much of it."

The voice of my mother, low and insistent, buzzed in my ears as I crossed the hallway: "What a thing to do, Isam! Tear up the letter? Couldn't you see how happy it made your father? And you go and tear it up?"

I paid no attention to her. I went on to my room and closed the door behind me. Then I sat down calmly at the desk, lit the lamp, took out a book, and started reviewing. I can still remember that the chapter that I read that night was "Osmotic Pressure": fluids move through the semi-permeable membrane and the exchange of fluids in either direction comes to an end when the pressure around the membrane is equalized. My father, Uncle Anwar, el-Ghamdi, the letter, and Farghal's beautiful handwriting—all these came into my mind from time to time as I read, like disconnected images that shone and then died out, but they didn't upset me. When I'm taken by surprise by something, my mind records its details precisely and it takes a little while before my rational faculties put everything in order again; that's when I react strongly. My reaction may be powerful, but it's delayed. I stopped reviewing at about three in the morning, and I could hear a distant din coming from the studio— voices, laughter, and music. I had undressed, put on my pajamas, and was ready to go to sleep when I heard heavy footsteps in the corridor, my father's footsteps. He drummed with his fingers on the door. I didn't answer. He opened the door slowly, peered in, smiled, and entered. I remained where I was, standing in front of the bed, and he approached and threw himself into the chair, stretching his legs out in front of him; from his face, whose details were illumined by the light of the desk lamp, he appeared to be both completely intoxicated and tired. A moment passed, and I sat down slowly on the bed. Suddenly my father said, "What time do you have lectures tomorrow?"

I replied, "Twelve o'clock."

Then he said, as though the times of the lectures were what really concerned him, "Excellent. You have a little time to sleep so that tomorrow you can go off refreshed."

Silence returned and I felt a sudden irritation and wished that my father would go and leave me alone, but he yawned and said, "You know, Isam, I'm very optimistic about your future. I'm sure you'll be a great scientist. I sense that you love your studies. Don't you love chemistry?"

There was a tone to his voice that increased my irritation but he continued, "I'm sure you love chemistry. How else could you be doing so well? The important thing, though, champ, is just to see it through. Right! Not just get your baccalaureate and take it easy. You have to get your PhD. In my day, the baccalaureate was a big deal, but now! You have to have at least a PhD before you can say you really did something. And anyway, what else do you have to do? You're not in a relationship with a girl and you're not in a hurry to get married. Aren't I right? Tell me. Tell me and don't be shy."

My father let out a laugh, and his playfulness seemed embarrassing and heavy. He resumed, apparently determined to be jolly, "Even if there is a girl on your mind, you can still go on with your studies. In fact, an early marriage might even motivate you to work harder. The important thing is that you shouldn't have any ambitions in the arts field. Art is the only thing I'm afraid of. You know, Isam, when I abandoned my studies, I didn't think for a minute. I felt I was doing something very natural. I have no regrets, of course. I've never regretted giving my life to art. I was incapable of imagining myself as anything else. True, things were often against me but I did what I had to. Before the Revolution I used to work at three newspapers, and people used to read and understand and compare. Any new artist who came up, people would see him and judge his talent. After nationalization, it became just a matter of earning a living. Sometimes it seems to me that neither people have the desire to laugh nor artists the desire to produce. The whole thing's turned into just a matter of doing what you have to. You draw a joke and you know it's stupid and people read it and know it's stupid, but they read it."

I prepared myself to ask my father to leave but couldn't.

"Did you see Shakir's cartoon in *al-Ahram* today?"*

"No."

"You have to see it. It's very strange. I don't what's happened to Shakir—has he gone nuts or what? Do you know what he drew today? A sun's disc with two lines coming out of it that he'd twisted round each other and underneath he'd written 'Knitting.' Get how dumb that is? It's supposed to be a joke and people expect to laugh when they read it. Laugh at what? At the artist's stupidity, of course. But Mr. Shakir is of course a well-known artist and *al-Ahram* pays him eight hundred pounds a month. Even if he turned in a few scribbles, no one could say anything. No, what matters is that Shakir thinks he's a great artist and if you run into him at the Journalists' Syndicate he pretends not to know you, or he'll remember you after a while and say, 'My dear friend! Please excuse me, but you've changed a lot and you know what my mind's like!' Of course, he doesn't try that stuff with me, of all people. He comes right over to me and minds his manners."

I couldn't stand it any more so I jumped up. My father seemed taken aback. There was a moment of silence. Then he got up from his chair and said as he turned to go out, just as though we'd just come to the end of an ordinary conversation on an ordinary night,

"Right. Well, I'll leave you to get some sleep. Good night."

---

* Al-Ahram *is Egypt's leading daily newspaper.*

He took some steps toward the door. I hung my head and looked at the interwoven colors of the design on the carpet and for a moment was overcome by an obscure feeling that my father hadn't left the room and that he'd come over to me—and when I raised my eyes, there he was standing in front of me, and he stretched out his hand without speaking, put it on my shoulder, looked at me for a moment, and then said, "I'm sorry, Isam."

❖

When your father is a weak sick old man who clings onto your hand as you walk down the street next to him, leaning his weight on you for fear of falling over, and the passersby stare at your father's infirmity and examine you with curious glances that come to rest on your face, how are you likely to feel? You may feel embarrassed at your father's weakness and you may exaggerate your display of concern so as to garner appreciative looks, or you may talk nastily and cruelly to him because you love him and are sad for his sake and you want him to go back to being the way he was, strong and capable.

Life comes out on Wednesdays and I went to the news vendor in front of the mosque to buy it but he didn't know of it, and I went to another vendor, in Giza Square, and to a third, and a fourth, and I took a bus to Suleiman Pasha Square and went to the big newsstand there and when the vendor approached me I asked him with a show of indifference, "Have you ever heard of a magazine called *Life*?"

I spoke to him like this because every time a vendor denied the existence of the magazine for which my father drew, I felt embarrassed and sad. I was expecting that this one wouldn't know it either and my seemingly indifferent question reduced my embarrassment and placed me and the vendor on the same side—as though I too, in spite of my question, was denying that any such magazine existed. The vendor, however, and to my surprise, knew it and said, "Fifteen piasters."

I felt relieved and paid the price, and I took the magazine and searched on the last page until I found my father's name. There was a small square with, at the bottom, the signature "Abd el-Ati." On the way home, I studied the cartoon. When I got to the house it was two o'clock in the afternoon and my father was still asleep, so I opened the door to his room and entered quietly. Then I swept aside the heavy black curtains and light flooded the space. My father opened his eyes and noticed me, and I said, smiling, "Good morning."

"Good morning, Isam. What time is it?"

I told him the time and he yawned, stretched his hand out to the bedside table, picked up a pack of cigarettes, lit one, and took a drag that turned into a fit of coughing. I took up a chair, came close, and sat myself in front of him, the magazine in my hand. Tapping it, I said, laughing, "Happy now, my dear sir? That cartoon you did today almost got me sent to the police station!"

Taken aback, my father asked what I meant, so I told him, "No big deal. I got into a fight with a friend of mine over what the cartoon meant." As I said this I straightened the edge of the carpet with my foot so that I seemed to be speaking about something quite incidental and ordinary that happened all the time.

"Good heavens! You got into a fight?" my father asked me in amazement.

"I want to ask you first. The man in the cartoon today, isn't he supposed to be Anwar Sadat?"

My father responded, "Yes. Absolutely."

I let out my breath as though relieved and said, "So I was right."

My father pulled himself up, rested his back against the head of the bed, and said, worry starting to appear in his eyes, "What's the story?"

"No big deal. As you know, they read *Life* at the university, so every Wednesday I have to have this quarrel with my friends. They all look at your cartoon and then they keep pestering me with questions about 'Does your father mean So-and-so or So-and-so?' Today, especially, if the drawing hadn't been Anwar Sadat, the meaning would have changed completely."

My father asked me, as he put on his glasses and looked anxiously at the drawing, "Aren't the features clear?"

I answered emphatically, "Of course. They're very clear. But this friend of mine, he's a communist and you know what adolescents the communists are. He insists you're a rightist and would never attack Sadat in your cartoons."

Thus I initiated a long discussion with my father on a topic over which we always disagreed, and which I knew well, even though he sometimes got angry with me and attacked me, made him happy. And in the evening, my father would complain about me to his friends, telling them about his discussion with me and describing me as being—like all my generation—irritable and conceited, and then insert rapidly into the middle

31

of what he was saying, "Just imagine, everyone! Isam tells me that they read *Life* at the university and that his colleagues got into a fight with him over today's cartoon."

Having slipped this sentence in, my father would quickly finish what he was saying, and I could almost feel his anxiety lest anyone disagree with him or call him a liar.

❖

It was summer and Ramadan, and the university was on vacation. Neither I nor my father fasted but we respected my mother's feelings and observed the Ramadan regime—breaking fast at sunset, eating again before sunrise. I had spent the night with my friends at el-Fishawi's café, which was crowded and noisy, and returned to the house at three in the morning. My father and mother were seated at the table. My mother was eating her predawn meal and my father was busy devouring a plate of cookies, with tea. I divined, from the looseness of his lips, his vacant look, and the way the crumbs dribbled onto his gallabiya, that he had been smoking hashish. I exchanged a few words with them in passing, then went into my room, and leafed through the newspapers for the coming day, which I had bought in el-Hussein. Then I slept and woke up in the morning to find someone frantically shaking my body. I opened my eyes and found my mother beating her cheeks and pulling at me to get up. I ran after her to my father's room. He lay naked on the bed and looked as though he was asleep, except that a mumbling sound was coming from his mouth and a feeble movement made his huge body tremble. There was an expression on his face that looked as though he was being pursued by a nightmare from which he was trying, unsuccessfully, to awake. My mother wailed out, "See your father, Isam!"

She bent over him, took him in her arms, and started calling to him. Then she buried her face in his chest and burst into tears. In an hour, the doctor came and, after examining my father carefully, bent down to me and informed me in a whisper that he had suffered an aneurysm. He advised me to take him immediately to the hospital, asked for twenty pounds, which he thrust into his pocket with thanks, and left. The ambulance workers exerted huge efforts with my mother before managing to get my father dressed in a white gallabiya and then they placed him on the stretcher and took him down the stairs, my mother and I behind them. As they took my father through the entryway of the building, Huda, our young maid, suddenly appeared and, with her skinny, nervy body and flying pigtail, started running after the stretcher and leaping round it and screaming.

In the light of the lamp suspended over the bed in the hospital, my father's face seemed to me to be divided into two halves, one with a bulging eye, opened as far as it could go and blood-shot, and the other defeated and sagging. My father was trying to speak and a vague, suppressed, rattling sound emerged from within him. My mother left me with him and went to ask the hospital administration about something. In the afternoon, friends, relatives, colleagues from work, and others I didn't know appeared. They spoke to us—my mother and me—of God's mercy, treatment overseas, and friends of theirs (people they knew very well) who had suffered exactly the same symptoms as my father's and who had recovered, with God's help, and now enjoyed the most robust health and happiness. Then the visitors went away, one by one, leaving behind bunches of roses and colored boxes of chocolates, and my mother and I remained seated in front of my father; and when he closed his bulging eye and his breathing became regular, I realized that he had gone to sleep. It was late, perhaps after midnight, when we heard a faint knocking on the door, which opened a little to reveal the face of Uncle Anwar. He was wearing his black working tuxedo with the shiny lapels and under it a white shirt and sagging black bowtie. Uncle Anwar's eyes roamed the room and then he signaled to me with his hand, so I went outside, followed by my mother, and he heard from us what had happened and asked us in detail about the opinions and prognoses of the doctors. His face was dark and the way he interrupted us as we spoke indicated that he was angry. Soon he put out his cigarette with his shoe and asked my mother if he could see him. He went forward, pushed open the door, and entered, and when he got close to my father I thought I saw a flash of consciousness pass quickly over my father's eyes, and that he recognized Anwar. This, however, was quickly extinguished and the eye resumed its vacant look. Uncle Anwar laughed loudly and said, "What's going on, my dear Mr. Abduh? What kind of a stunt is this you're trying to pull? Do you get a kick out of making us worry or what? Look at you—as strong as a bull! These guys sent people to look for me at a wedding and they told me, 'Come to Abduh at once!' So I thought something bad must have happened!"

He turned to my mother and went on, "What kind of way to behave is that, Madam? You gave me a nasty shock. There's nothing wrong with Abduh. Look at him! He's as strong as a horse."

Then he turned back to my father, seemingly wanting to empty out everything he had to say at one go, or having decided not to stay silent for a second.

"That's enough now, Abduh! As a punishment for having got me worried, I'm going to come see you on Tuesday and the bill's on you—you're going to pay for a bottle of Forty-eight brandy and a kilo of kebab. Isam and the madam are my witnesses."

I could almost have sworn that my father's face jerked into something like a smile. Uncle Anwar went on talking and laughing and then said goodbye to my father and us and went out. I followed him but when he passed through the door that led to the hospital's lobby, he didn't look at me but turned to the right where the elevator was. Soon, however, he slowed his steps, then stood and bent forward, putting his hands over his face as gasps of violent weeping escaped.

The morning of the following day, one of the nurses at the hospital got into a resounding fight with the cleaner, accusing him openly of stealing the patients' food. The cleaner shouted filthy insults and leaped forward in an attempt to strike the nurse, but colleagues gathered around and prevented him, and at the moment they were sitting him down on a chair and starting to calm him down, my father died.

❖ 4 ❖

I got my baccalaureate in science and was appointed as a researcher in the government's Chemistry Authority. The appointment suited my circumstances: at that time I was making continuous and exhausting efforts to realize my withdrawal from society, in which context it was enough for me to become acquainted with one intelligent individual for my mission to be aborted, since, when this happened, I would ask myself, "Why am I putting up with all this pain in the cause of cutting myself off from people when there is among them at least one person intelligent enough to understand me?" From this perspective, my presence in the Chemistry Authority served to hasten my withdrawal. The building was ancient, shabby, and covered in dust. It had been erected in a forgotten corner of Ramses Street where, for the length of its fifty years, a clamorous life had swirled around it while it crouched in the silence of death.

You may use your bathroom at home for many a year without it occurring to you that there is a kind of life that goes on inside the drain. If, however, at some point, you were to perform an experiment and raise the cover, a whole world would appear to your eyes—dozens of maggots, and insects of different kinds, eating, multiplying, fighting, and killing one another. You would then be struck with amazement by the notion that these creatures had been living with you for years without your knowledge. This was the image that haunted me every morning as I walked among the crowds on Ramses Street, with all its bustle and noise, then turned to the left and abandoned it to enter the Chemistry Authority—a drain in whose darkness and damp were enclosed a group of filthy cockroaches of the sort that when stepped on and crushed extrude a sticky white liquid. 'Cockroaches'—that was the scientific term for my colleagues in the Authority. My boss, Dr. Sa'id, didn't, in fact, have a doctorate, though he had taken the exams three times in succession and failed, leading the Authority employees to award him the title (either as a compliment or sarcastically) and he had immediately grabbed on to it and would get angry if he were not so addressed. The worst troubles to disturb the tranquility of this man who occupied the post of Head of the Research Department (a post, that is to say, of some moment) were those that afflicted him after a meal. At midmorning, Dr. Sa'id would sit himself down at his desk and devour a large dish overflowing with stewed broad beans, bean patties, and fried eggs, accompanied by sweet red onions and pickled eggplant, after finishing which he would be compelled to loosened the belt of his pants to alleviate the pressure on his great belly. Then he would gulp down a glass of imported Epsom salts and send someone off for tea. His head was bald, without a single hair, and this made him look as though he were sick or wearing a disguise, and one's first glance at him, with his bulging eyes, sparse eyebrows, sagging dewlaps, and vulgar voice, left a bestial impression. Sometimes, as I observed him, a strange idea would occur to me: in some mysterious way, I expected that Dr. Sa'id would suddenly interrupt what he was saying and reveal his true nature, i.e., bellow and pull his tail out for all of us to see and place it on the desk in front of him. I knew very well of course that such a thing would never happen but if it had I wouldn't have been that surprised. During the tea break, all the employees of the department would come to Dr. Sa'id's office to pay their respects and hover around him, passing the time in conversation until they had to go. Three topics were dear to the doctor's heart—the national soccer championships since he was a loyal Ahli Club fan, the automobile market since he made money dealing in cars on the side, and, most importantly, sex, its secrets and its arts, since he was an outrageous skirt-chaser.* Some said that the reason for this was that his wife was frigid but he didn't have the guts to divorce her or take another wife because she was rich and supported him. This, supposedly, was why he satisfied his lusts far from home, in his office at the Chemistry Authority. Dr. Sa'id was particularly smitten with the department's cleaning women and female workers—a taste no doubt attributable to his early experiences. When one of these women pleased him, he would keep calling her to his office, where he would treat her quite informally and press gifts on her until, little by little, he'd start coming on to her by making jokes of a sexual nature, which he'd toss out to her quite confidently, roaring with laughter. When the day came for him to make his move, Dr. Sa'id would invite the woman to his office and order her to close the door (which had a special lock that could not be opened from the outside). After she'd closed the door, he'd ask her to get something from the cupboard, and then he'd get up and place himself behind her and stick his huge body against her back, hugging her and having his way her. When this was going on in the office, the workers in the unit would know and would whisper and gossip and laugh about it, or express their disapproval. Under no circumstances, however, would they express their opposition openly.

Years passed and Dr. Sa'id practiced his private life at the research unit in peace. Only once did something happen to disturb its even tenor, which was when Umm Imad

---

* Ahli is Egypt's leading soccer club, with a massive popular following.

appeared in the department—a beautiful young woman with green eyes who'd moved from Tanta after her husband died and joined the department as a worker on a temporary contract. Dr. Sa'id fancied Umm Imad from the first day. He promised her he'd do his best to get her appointed on a permanent contract and started arriving every morning at the department with his pockets full of different kinds of chewing gum and candies that he gave to Umm Imad for her children. Did Dr. Sa'id make his move too early or had he misjudged her from the beginning? He called for her and ordered her to close the door and she closed it. As usual he got up and tried to stick himself against her but she put up serious resistance. He didn't care and tried to get closer and she growled warningly, in a voice that was clear but still not loud, "Shame on you!" Wisdom required that he desist, but he kept on going, either because he was so aroused or because all he saw in her refusal was a crass kind of coquetry. He threw himself on her with his whole body and put his arms around her, but she screamed and went on screaming, her cries resounding through the Research Unit. In a second, the employees had gathered outside the office and when the screaming went on, one of them plucked up his courage and knocked on the glass pane in the door. Minutes of silence passed. Then Dr. Sa'id's heavy footsteps were heard and he himself opened the door to them and they burst inside, hoping for the scene of a lifetime. Umm Imad stood in front of the cupboard, struggling to catch her breath, her hair disheveled and her gallabiya pulled tight and torn in more than one place. Everything about her indicated that a violent struggle had just taken place and she started

39

repeating in a tearful voice, clasping her head with her hands as though lamenting at a funeral, "Shame on you! I'll make you pay for this, you'll see. Do you think if I was that kind of woman I'd be living the way I do? But the Lord knows all. I work to take care of my children. Shame on you!"

For one minute, or two, Umm Imad was on the verge of having an effect on the employees, but Dr. Sa'id recovered his poise, lit a cigarette, went up to Umm Imad, and took a strong grip on her shoulder. Then his angry voice rang out like thunder while he waggled his middle finger in a vulgar gesture.

"Listen, you silly little girl! Keep that stuff for saints' carnivals! 'Woooooh! Blessings, Holy Master! Wooooooh!' I'm no fairground sucker and I'm not some dumb wog. Forget the 'This happened and then that happened'—I know how that crap works. I'm telling you for the last time, in front of these men, you either return the hundred pounds that were in the drawer or I call the police, I swear. Got it?"

There were exclamations and whispers as the employees listened first to Dr. Sa'id's version of events and then to Umm Imad's, and there was some attempt to bring about a quick reconciliation, but Dr. Sa'id refused. He refused the very idea and shouted at them, "What? What's going on here, my friends? Is a hundred pounds a joke to you? You want my supplementary benefits to go for nothing?" He struck one palm on the other and muttered furiously, "That's the limit!"

Umm Imad swore by the greatest oaths and prayed she be struck blind and her son Imad run over by a streetcar if she'd touched or even set eyes on the money but in vain.

Dr. Sa'id continued to insist that she return the money that
he'd been paid the day before, left forgotten in the drawer,
and not found this morning after Umm Imad had cleaned
the room. The employees were all well aware of the truth but
they made a silent pact to respect Dr. Sa'id's version and
oppose Umm Imad, feeling that a victory for Umm Imad
over Dr. Sa'id would be, in some sense, a defeat for them
too. The following day, delegations went to her to scare her,
force her to accept a reconciliation, and return the money
but she seemed to have lost her wits and kept screaming and
cursing herself and swearing on the Qur'an. The business
ramified and meetings were convened and broke up and the
problem kept the employees busy for a whole week until,
finally, they were successful and Umm Imad, pushed by
the others, went to Dr. Sa'id's office, apologized, and
kissed his head; indeed, she would have kissed his hand
had he not pulled it back and declared in front of everyone,
in a tone of voice indicating the opposite, that Umm Imad
had stolen nothing, that he'd found the money where he'd
forgotten it in the pocket of his jacket, and that Umm Imad
in fact was a very decent woman, one whom he loved like his
own daughter. I was present and at the moment when Abd
el-Alim, the office messenger, proposed that everyone recite
the first chapter of the Qur'an to bless the reconciliation, I
felt that what was happening in front of me was not real, that
the people seated there—Dr. Sa'id, Umm Imad, and the
employees—were all actors who were playing out a well-
rehearsed scene after which they would straightaway take off
their costumes and resume their original characters. This
strange idea of mine must have been apparent on my face

because I noticed that everyone avoided looking at me when they were speaking. I had no doubt that my colleagues hated me and longed for an opportunity to do me harm.

From my first day in the department, I had determined to despise and look down on them. Without saying anything, I knew how to let them feel their insignificance. It happened at this period that I needed glasses and I picked out round frames made of thin plastic. I felt that these gave my face a superior cast that was somehow provocative. Every morning I'd go to my office with the newspapers under my arm and a huge book that I chose deliberately as one that I knew no one in the office would ever have heard of—el-Isfahani's *Songs*, or Gibbon's *Decline and Fall of the Roman Empire*, or Oswald Spengler's *Decline of the West*. Once I'd done with the newspapers, I'd open my huge tome and immerse myself in my reading. When the room filled up with employees and the noise level grew, I'd raise my head from the book and give those present a steady stare, without speaking. The noise would then die down right away and sometimes they'd withdraw from the room.

I resolutely refused their insistent attempts to get closer to me, to find some common factor, and when any of the employees came up to me smiling and asked me hesitantly, "What are you reading, Mr. Isam?" I'd answer him seriously and without pausing, "To tell you the truth this book is extremely specialized. You'd find it difficult to understand." Then I'd start reading again and he'd retire, silenced.

After a month in the department, I could almost touch their hatred for me with my hands. Dr. Sa'id treated me with caution. I could see dislike and alarm in his eyes. For him, I was something mysterious that he feared and knew was superior to him. One morning, he came to me, reproached me laughingly for not coming to see him in his office like the rest of my coworkers, and said, "My dear man, do come and drink a glass of tea with us. They're a nice bunch and we keep ourselves entertained."

A malicious pleasure filled me, because he'd provided me with a perfect opportunity to give him a slap in the face. I looked at him seriously, as though I hadn't understood. Then I told him quietly, resuming my reading, "I don't have time for entertainment."

From the corner of my eye, I saw his face darken with anger and he said as he left the room, "Fine. Don't come. I shouldn't have asked. Do you think we have nothing better to do? We're up to our necks in work."

It occurred to me then that he wouldn't let my slight pass unpunished and that a tough battle was inevitable. And I was right.

❖

During the month of Ramadan, Dr. Sa'id transformed himself into a pious believer. His long green string of prayer beads never left his hand, he covered his bald patch with a crocheted white skullcap, and on his feet he wore open sandals from which his thick swollen toes with their horny nails protruded. He spent his days between his office and the bathroom, where he would repeat his ablutions, and he kept up a flow of "Glory be to God!"'s, leading the employees in their prayers with strict punctuality, and reciting the Qur'an to himself from a large copy that he kept open in front of him on his desk.

On the first day of Ramadan, I sat down at my desk, opened the papers, and started reading. As was my custom every morning, I asked Abd el-Alim to get me a cup of coffee. I noticed that he seemed reluctant and was muttering something in a low voice but I paid no attention and went back to reading. Half an hour went by and Abd el-Alim did not turn up with the coffee. When he came in on some other errand I questioned him and he answered insolently, "No coffee today. Season's greetings. Happy Ramadan."

Before I could respond, he went on quickly, "It's Dr. Sa'id's instructions. No coffee or tea during Ramadan."

Abd el-Alim was an aged peasant, from Minuf. He spied on the employees and passed on information to Dr. Sa'id. Like the rest, he hated me and the pleasure he took in getting his revenge was obvious from his tone of voice, because he was a servant and servants derive an ecstatically malicious pleasure from seeing one of their masters in a position of weakness.

I looked at him in exasperation and was on the verge of calling him names and ordering him to make the coffee and let whatever might happen happen when I thought better of it, lit a cigarette, and went back to reading.

That night I stayed awake until the call for the dawn prayer was given. I was so furious I couldn't get to sleep. The idea that that animal Sa'id should evaluate my conduct and control my behavior, and that the ignoramuses and servants of the department should treat me cheekily, filled me with gall.

The morning of the following day, I determined on a course of action. I asked the maid, Huda, to make me a thermos full of coffee, took the flask under my arm, and marched in, ready for a fight. On reaching my room, I found stuck up on the door a piece of paper on which I read, "Gentlemen members of the Research Department are kindly requested to refrain from partaking of drinks during the month of Exalted Ramadan out of respect for the feelings of those fasting. Signed: The Administration." I recognized Dr. Sa'id's handwriting so I put out my hand, tore the piece of paper violently down, squashed it into a ball, and threw it on the floor, looking around in search of one of them with whom to initiate battle, but the corridor was deserted. I went into the office, poured myself a cup of coffee, and lit a cigarette. I tried to read the newspapers but was incapable of concentrating I was so excited. I could sense the coming confrontation and was trying to hasten it along. I would teach that mule a lesson he'd never forget, I thought to myself, and I pictured myself throwing him to the ground and my shoe pummeling his bald head with kicks until the blood flowed.

After half an hour I heard the sound of footsteps in the corridor and soon Dr. Sa'id appeared at the door to the room, Abd el-Alim behind him. Sa'id looked at the cigarette in my hand and said in a loud voice, "What's this, Isam? What's going on? This is quite unacceptable."

"What's unacceptable?" I asked him in a voice shaking with excitement.

Dr. Sa'id's voice rose even higher.

"My dear friend, 'If you must do ill, then conceal your-selves.' Are you or are you not a Muslim?"

"Not."

"What?" Dr. Sa'id said in astonishment.

45

"Didn't you just ask me if I'm a Muslim? Now I've told you—I'm not. I am not a Muslim."

"So what are you?"

"What business is it of yours?"

A moment of silence elapsed. Then Sa'id advanced a few steps and his voice rang out in fury: "No, now you've gone too far. Listen to me, my fine friend. I don't intend to get into a slanging match with you out of respect for the Noble Month, but just remember you're talking to your administrative director. Do you understand me?"

My body was quivering with rage and I said nothing but I stood up and stared into his face with fury, while he smiled mockingly, wagged a finger at me, and said, "Plus, can you tell me why a big boy like you can't manage to fast?"

"He's sure to have a valid excuse, doctor!"* exclaimed one of the employees who had gathered behind Dr. Sa'id, and a few laughs rang out. I was so angry I lost my wits and found myself striking the thermos, which fell to the ground making a great clatter, and the top came off and the coffee poured out over the floor. The employees took a few steps back and were startled into silence, and I shouted with the full force of my anger, "You make fun of me, you imbeciles? You understand nothing."

My outburst took them aback for a moment, and then the same employee, who was called Ahmad Guda, called out, "Of course not. You're the one that knows it all, Mr. Know-It-All."

---

* Muslims are excused from the fast in Ramadan in cases of travel or illness; in addition, Muslim women are excused while pregnant, nursing, or menstruating. As an off-color joke, the employee is insinuating that Isam is experiencing the last.

Some of those who were standing there laughed and Guda clapped his hands and said, in a silly, drawn out voice, "Mr. Knooooooooow-It-All!" The raucous laughter grew and I yelled at them, my voice lost in the noise, "Go ahead! Laugh! I've read more about Islam than any of you."

They didn't listen to me and the laughter continued. I got the impression that the way I looked when I was shouting at them increased their mirth, and my indignation flared back up and I screamed at them, "Idiots! Trash!"

The laughter came to an immediate stop. Whispers ran around and Dr. Sa'id exclaimed, coming up to me, "Shut your mouth!"

"Shut your own mouth, you animal! You're just trash and you know nothing!"

They were shocked. Silence reigned for a moment. Then suddenly Abd el-Alim rushed at me, hand raised, and screamed hoarsely, "Blasphemer! Dog!"

All I have after that is confused impressions. Abd el-Alim launched himself at me and I tried to slap him on the face but my hand missed and hit his neck. He grabbed me by my shirt and started shouting abuse at me and the employees separated us and dragged me by force out of the room, Dr. Sa'id's deep voice following me as he shouted, "See, he's a communist! A communist! I had my suspicions from the beginning. Refer him for investigation immediately!"

❖ 5 ❖

To look at, a drop of water is as pure and transparent as crystal, but if you magnify it under a lens, a thousand impurities appear. The moon is beautiful and unsullied as long as it's far away, but if you get close it looks like a filthy, deserted beach. Even the face of the one you love, whose fresh, rosy complexion captivates your heart, appears—as soon as you have learned to see it properly—like ugly, wrinkled cloth. You can test this truth every time. Our love of beauty is merely a trick produced by the way we look, and the broader the vision grows the clearer the wrinkles are seen.

❖ 6 ❖

Our house—forties style; high, decorated ceilings; large floor tiles with small squares, their colors worn away by people's feet; sedate wooden furniture with an old smell; chair covers and table cloths whose color had changed and which had worn through in several places from age. Our house had spacious echoing rooms, large balconies looking out over the street and other, narrower ones, at the sides, a large bathroom for the masters and another small one, tucked away, for the servants and emergencies, and two separate entrances—one for the family and another that opened directly onto the sitting room, which my father had turned into his studio. Everything in our house invoked a rich former life that was now on its last legs. After my father's death, I moved into his studio. I left everything as it was—the paintings stacked next to the wall, the cans of paint, the palette, the little stool, the place where the friends had sat, the small cushions and the rug; even the goza, the brazier, and the bags of charcoal I left in their places. All I did was to make myself a space in the far corner of the room, where I set up a camp bed to sleep on. Each night, before closing them, my eyes would roam over the studio. It was my father's place and I could feel his presence in a vague but definite way. I slept next to his things to guard them. When, one day, he came back, he would find everything as he had left it and I would go back to my old room. My sick mother slept in one room in the apartment and in another my grandmother, who was over eighty. The maid Huda would put her bedding down in the passage between the two rooms, hugging her baby girl, and sleep. Huda had married a plumber who had gone to Iraq to work two years previously and no more had been heard of him, so she had returned to our house to serve us. My uncle—my mother's only brother—had spent ten years in Saudi Arabia and therefore supported us all—me, my mother, my grandmother, Huda, and her daughter. We were a tight-knit family in the old style, but I drew close and saw.

❖ 7 ❖

I returned one day from the department to find my mother silent and anxious.

When I questioned her closely, she cried and said that she was afraid but wouldn't elaborate. Huda made a sign to me behind her back and took me aside in the kitchen and informed me that my mother was afraid because she had a lump in her chest. The swelling had appeared several months earlier but she'd decided to tell no one and had tried to treat it on her own. She'd tried everything. She'd rubbed her chest with dough, she'd put a poultice on it, and she'd dressed it with water and sugar. She'd even taken birth-control pills, on the advice of a woman living nearby, and in the end, when these methods had failed, my mother had decided to ignore the swelling—to talk, laugh, get mad, and live as though it didn't exist. A faint hope told her that she would wake up one morning and discover that the swelling had disappeared as suddenly as it had come. In vain, however. The swelling had come precisely to stay, invade, and spread, and when it reached her neck and this puffed up and became covered with blue lines, it became impossible to hide or ignore it.

In the evening, the doctor's clinic was crowded with patients and their families. I could distinguish the sick from their relatives at one glance, not just from their pallor and fatigue but from their eyes, which had an absent look and seemed to be covered by a cloud, as though, when they looked in your direction, they saw something behind you—something obscure that only became visible a little before death.

The doctor was a professor of oncology and at the same time a brigadier general in the armed forces and religious (in the middle of his forehead there was a black mark caused by his prostrating himself and touching his head to the ground in prayer, while over his head on the wall was the Throne Verse done in beautiful gilded script). After examining my mother carefully, he went back to his desk and opened the conversation with the words "In the name of God the Merciful, the Compassionate." Then, bowing his head so that his eyes shouldn't meet hers, he said to my mother, "Hagga, you are a believer in God, and the Almighty has said in his Noble Book, *Naught shall visit us but what God has prescribed for us* (God has spoken the truth). I am sorry to have to tell you that you are afflicted with widespread malignant tumors. We call this type 'fourth-degree' and, unfortunately, they cannot be removed surgically. We place great hope in chemotherapy and yet greater hope in God, Almighty and Glorious."

In college, my professors used to conduct their experiments on rats, after first killing them. When the rat's turn came and the professor's huge hand, enclosed in its white glove, stretched down into the cage to grab it, it would try desperately to escape from his grip; and when it finally failed and the hand got a good grip on it and brought it out of the cage to kill it, the rat would let out an intermittent screech and spontaneously void its bowels. My mother screamed in the doctor's clinic and beat her cheeks and threw herself on the floor and the doctor and I only succeeded in calming her after some effort. He wrote out a list of tests and medications and I went home with her in a taxi. I didn't speak on the way back but gathered from a flash of light on her face in the darkness and from a sob that escaped her that she was crying. As soon as we reached the house, my mother phoned her brother Abbas; as she told him an expression of anguish sketched itself on her face that never again left her.

Months of treatment went by. My mother's body grew emaciated, her breasts were altogether destroyed, her skin darkened, and her hair fell out, but the anguish never left her eyes for a second. A sense of foreboding that could not be stilled took possession of her and she came to be dominated by a single idea—that she must drive death away at any price, escape the looming grasp, and live. I read once that when an elephant feels it is going to die, it walks to the place it has chosen to be its grave. There the elephant stops and calmly awaits its end. What nobler thing is there than to be brave and never snap? I was my mother's only son and she loved me, I know; and I also know that if she were to choose between my death and her total cure, she would choose my death, unhesitatingly—and let it sadden her afterward as it might, so long as she was safe and sound.

My mother's terror of death left her with no concern to spare for anything else. When my uncle Abbas came to visit us, she would go to even greater lengths to show off her weakness and powerlessness. She would make up to him, passionately praying to God on his behalf that He increase his wealth and preserve his children. She would caress his chest with her hands in false affection and yell angrily into my face—since what then could be my worth?—that I'd left the window open and the cold air might do my uncle harm. When he got up to leave, my mother would burst into tears and tell him that she was afraid all the nagging by 'the bastards' (meaning his wife) would one day harden his heart against her. At this my uncle would smile, bend over and kiss her brow, produce from his pocket the envelope of money that he had got ready beforehand, and then whisper to her anxiously as he thrust the envelope under her pillow, "Whatever happens, please don't say anything to my wife Hikmat about my coming to see you because you know she's getting old and bad tempered and I don't need more problems."

❖

I was having sex with the maid Huda. Desire would gnaw at me, playing such havoc with my nerves that I would forget the smell of sweat emanating from her body, her thick, coarse hands, and her ugly, brown, cracked toenails. I'd call her and she'd know what I wanted from my tone of voice and come to my room, closing the door behind her and waiting in silence without looking at me. I'd pounce and put my arms around her and everything would happen quickly and without a word. I'd be desperate to get it over with and when we were finished, she'd slip out of my grasp and gather up her clothes, leaving me feeling empty inside as the details of the encounter sank in, stripped of the clamor of pleasure, so that I felt the same disgust that I had felt during my college days when my hand touched the sticky, slime-covered belly of a frog, and I would try to rid myself of it with a hot shower.

At the beginning of our relationship, I used to make sure that my mother was asleep before calling Huda to my room. After a while, I no longer bothered. My mother knew what was going on and didn't care or, at the least, didn't dare to object because she needed Huda constantly. Huda it was who fed her, washed her body, changed her clothes, went with her to the toilet, and had learned by heart the times for all her different medications.

After a session with Huda, I'd go out and find my mother sitting in bed, all eyes. She'd always open a conversation or ask a question designed to reject the notion that she had any idea of what had just happened in my room. When sometimes I complained to my mother that Huda was neglecting my things and hint that I was thinking of getting rid of her, she'd look at me with terrified eyes and say, "Never mind! I'll send her today to clean your room."

I was certain that what she meant was that she'd send her to me to have sex with. My mother couldn't imagine her life without Huda, and the thought that anyone might make her mad enough to leave the house terrified her. She would have liked her to leave everything else and sit by her all day and all night. She trembled with fright at the idea that one day she might need Huda and not find her, and when Huda was obliged to neglect her to take care of her baby girl, Kawsar—when she went to feed or change her—I could feel my mother's terrible resentment at the situation. Once Kawsar got sick and had a high temperature so I gave Huda ten pounds to take her to the doctor but my mother objected and made out that it wasn't important, insisting that children often got fevers that went away on their own without treatment and without doing any harm. Huda was almost convinced that there was no point in going to the doctor and wouldn't have done so if I hadn't insisted. When in the end Huda left with her daughter and my mother and I were alone together, she scolded me for insisting. I answered her that children needed care and that the fever could be a symptom of a serious illness. My mother was silent for a moment and put her finger in her mouth (a habit she'd acquired along with her illness); then she looked at me with a terrified and evil expression on her face and whispered, "Just think, Isam! If our Lord were to rid Huda of that girl of hers, she'd really be free to look after me."

I muttered something in disavowal, not believing my ears, but my mother turned her face as far away from me as she could, made a gesture with her hand, and said as though making light of it, "What's so bad about that? Lots of babies die. It'd just be one more gone to join the rest."

❖ 8 ❖

Huda, who was deposited as a baby in front of an orphanage, taken as a child by a lady from Alexandria to work in her house, inured to having her arms and chest branded with a heated spoon for the least mistake or carelessness; Huda, the traces of whose early sufferings made her look in the incandescence of pleasure like a stray dog devouring, with a mixture of impatience and disbelief, some food it has come across unexpectedly—it was this Huda's fate to rule over us all, myself, my mother, and my grandmother, grasping our will in her fingers and squeezing. Sometimes (after I had had her and satisfied my needs) I would get mad at her and shout reproaches at her, as masters are supposed to do with their maids, at which point she would kill my anger with a single look and I would have to try calmly to make her understand her mistake. Her look would tell me, "Have you forgotten?" Sometimes she would make me rue my anger for a whole week, or two: I'd call her to my room and she'd come in and close the door and stand there; but when I started in on her, she'd push me resolutely away and leave with a killingly quiet step that set my desire on fire. Once her refusal of me lasted more than a month and I ended up begging her to allow me. Begging her! She looked at me for a while to register her victory over me for the last time and then let me use her body. At night, my mother would call Huda to take her to the bathroom; this might happen two or three times in one night. Sometimes Huda would pretend that she was asleep and couldn't hear and my mother would go on calling, holding in her urine and suffering and calling, and when in the end my mother started weeping as she begged, Huda would arise from her repose with the leisureliness of a goddess and take my mother to the bathroom. Despite her years, my mother didn't dare to blame her; on the contrary, she would receive her with a flood of blessings. That left my grandmother, and her Huda would scold in front of everyone, my mother usu-

55

ally joining in. My grandmother had reached eighty and so no one loved her any more, for kind feelings also have an allotted life and wither and fade, and one's survival beyond one's expected span somehow provokes people. No doubt my mother and my Uncle Abbas, thirty or forty years ago, used to love grandmother a lot, and to think, despite themselves, of the day on which she would die and how they would then mourn her for ages. But that sad day was delayed until they could feel the approach of their own ends, while my grandmother squatted there, unbudged by death.

Their response to this uncomfortable fact was to ignore her. Their ignoring of her was a punishment they imposed on my grandmother for still being there. My Uncle Abbas would sit with my mother for ages, talking, laughing, and drinking tea, and never once turn to where my grandmother lay in the same room. He had completely lost his awareness of her presence and my grandmother would remain in the middle of the laughter and talk, lying on her bed, silent, staring at the ceiling through her crooked glasses and with eyes over which the cataracts of age had crept. She might lie there for hours and then suddenly do something, like ask the others a question attributable to her weak powers of concentration and her scattered thoughts. It might be the hottest part of the summer and my grandmother would ask my mother to cover her with a blanket because she felt cold. Sometimes she would address my Uncle Abbas as though he were Huda, and sometimes she would try to get out of bed and fail and keep trying until she almost fell over. Then someone would have to jump up and help her, my aged grandmother's aim being to spread anxiety and spoil the atmosphere that had been created without her, to remind those present that she was old and weak and in need of a care that was not forthcoming because they were shirking their duties. Some months previously, my grandmother had started to wet herself, and my uncle had brought a doctor to solve this new problem. After examining my grandmother, the doctor came out, and I could tell from his face that he understood nothing. "Old age," he said. "There is no treatment." Then he prescribed her a medication of which seven drops were to be given her every night with a dropper. Before Huda gave it to my grandmother, my mother yelled at her vehemently, "Don't put seven. Give her ten, or twelve. Make her stop all that nastiness of hers."

The times that my grandmother chose to wet herself were carefully timed—such as in front of visitors, whether relatives or strangers. Right at the moment when the conversation was getting enjoyable and the visitors had settled themselves into their seats, my grandmother would suddenly urinate and discomfort and depression would reign. Once a young woman relative of ours called Nadia was visiting when she saw my grandmother get up, an expression of tranquility clothing her ancient features, and then bend her head like a guilty child while the urine poured down, soaking her clothes and streaming over the floor.

When Nadia beheld this, she stared for a moment as though she didn't understand, then burst into hot, vehement tears, and my mother and Huda got furious with my grandmother. Their cries mixed but my mother's voice was louder and she could be heard saying, "Shame on you, woman! We've been telling you to go to the damned bathroom since the morning."

Between my mother with her cancer, drawn and terrified of death, and my aged grandmother there existed a bitter animosity that may have been an indicator of ancient love and deep sorrow—a hopeless, vicious conflict of tooth and claw between two people imprisoned in the same narrow cell for too long after having lost all hope of release. When my mother rained insults and curses on her, I would think I caught sight of a slight tremor affecting my grandmother's tranquil face. There can be no doubt that she was angered by the lack of respect with which she was treated and she knew how to pay my mother back for her cruelty with skill. Once my mother and my grandmother were alone together in the house and my grandmother seized her opportunity. By this time all my mother's hair had fallen out because of the cancer medication and she covered her bald head with a headscarf, which slipped off easily, revealing the surface of her smooth dark pate with its flaking skin. My grandmother got out of bed, without assistance from anyone, and crossed the corridor to my mother's room with slow heavy footsteps that could easily be heard. When she entered the room, my mother screamed at her, "What do you want?"

My grandmother didn't reply but went up to my mother, on her face a deeply engrossed smile of the sort that appears on that of a child as it approaches an exciting toy that inspires feelings of both danger and pleasure. She came closer until she was next to my prone mother, ignoring her ever-louder cries, bent over her, stretched out her hand, and pulled the headscarf off her head, leaving it naked. Then she looked at my mother and said in clear tones, "Heavens! Where did all your hair go?"

When I went in to her a few moments later, my mother was howling with tears and screaming, "What's kept you alive so long? Just die! Just die and give us some peace!"

I watched my grandmother quit the room with the same heavy steps, leaving the storm behind her, and I noticed at that moment, on her aged face, the signs of satisfaction and contentment.

❖ 9 ❖

I have drawn close and seen, and I am neither sad nor happy. How do you feel when you examine your features closely in the mirror? A certain astonishment at the details of your face that you are seeing for the first time in close up. But your face, nose, eyes, eyebrows, and mouth confirm to you that your face is different from those of others.

That is how I feel about myself now. I have grasped the truth. I have taken it in my hand and it has sentenced me to loneliness. Isolation has become my fate because I have understood. It is not easy to achieve isolation and it does not come quickly. I have tried hard. I made many attempts and failed before I finally triumphed. A forbidding transparent wall that permits only seeing has been erected and I have withdrawn within my borders. I am possessed by the calm of the scientist who mixes solutions in test tubes and waits to record the reaction with precision and objectivity in his little notebook.

I am not now for or against anything. I am totally alone and being alone fills me with satisfaction and comfort. I am no longer concerned to prove my superiority or to make others aware of their inferiority. The days of quarrels and problems are past. I wake up every morning, pick up my books, go to the department, and sign in for the day as though I were in my own private office. I make tables for the readings and carry them out, starting with the newspapers, then a magazine, then a chapter from Nietzsche or Spengler. I may finish off the day with Shakespeare or an Arabic novel. The employees rarely speak to me. After my quarrel with Dr. Sa'id, they realized that I was special and too much for them to deal with for, were they to do so, it would push them toward unfamiliar and painful patterns of thought. It followed that they took a silent collective decision with regard to me— to resume the life that they knew and leave me alone in my dark obscure corner. They remember me sometimes when one of the women employees gives birth or a man marries and their colleagues subscribe to buy a present, sending me the messenger Abd el-Alim, who now speaks to me entirely politely. Sometimes it seems to me when I direct a look at him that a slight quiver afflicts his face and that he expects me to erupt at any moment and throw something at him. I suppress my smile at this thought and pay the amount requested without a word and go back to my reading. Isolation is my blessing, and I insist on preserving it. When night comes, I make my way to my father's studio and lock myself in.

Sometimes I go days without seeing my mother and I pay no attention to what goes on in the house. Even Huda I only rarely desire, passion being a part of the life from which I have withdrawn. In my father's studio I have fashioned for myself my own alternate world, a just and beautiful world to which I flee each night like a terrified child taking refuge in his mother's bosom, eagerly breathing in her good smell and complaining and crying until, calmed and reassured, he goes to sleep—my own beautiful world, enveloped in a cloud of hashish like a rose enveloped in its calyx. Hashish is a just ruler. He grants you whatever you deserve and gives to each his rights. On the simple, hashish bestows hilarious joy. As for the thinker, the one whose love of the truth is known to Sultan Hashish, he takes him by the hand, draws him close, and reveals secrets. As its acrid taste burns my throat and the effect begins to spread, I roam beyond new horizons and I learn. The truth is one and sempiternal and from it different scattered forms are born that are linked by fragile threads that cannot be seen from afar. I read about Hamlet, Ali ibn Abi Talib, Socrates, Eva Peron, Jehan Sadat, Aisha bint Abi Bakr, ancient Rome, Baghdad, and New York.* Read what you want, draw close and gaze, and the connecting threads become visible to you and the reality of a wonderful unity is revealed to you. From time to time, I have breakfast with my mother. I look on as, with bestial greed, she devours four spoons of honey, then drinks a glass of milk and eats a plate of eggs. My mother talks to me about the mistakes doctors make in diagnosis and asserts that our forefathers didn't know disease because they used to feed themselves well. She smiles imploringly and says, "You know, Isam, I don't believe a word of what the doctor says! I don't have cancer and I'll live to see him buried, the bastard."

Then she laughs hard and looks at my face from under her eyelids and I realize that were I to disagree with her or appear sad or even smile in pity, I would be cutting a fine thread that still connects her to some vague hope. I watch

---

* *Ali ibn Abi Talib was the cousin and son-in-law of the Prophet Muhammad; Aisha bint Abi Bakr was the second wife of the Prophet, after the death of his first wife Khadija.*

her laugh in silence and register in my brain in large letters, "Our abject greed for life is a truly contemptible thing." Imagine an efficient, energetic employee who loves his work. He makes a salary of a hundred pounds. He has never neglected his work for a single day and he has never been guilty of a lapse. One morning, however, he is surprised to find that his boss, for no reason other than his desire to do so, has reduced his salary to just ten pounds. What would you call such an employee if he didn't leave the job? Wouldn't he be contemptible if he continued to work for ten pounds and pretended to his boss that he was content and happy?

If my mother were to take her headscarf off in front of the mirror and look at her head and her drawn, exhausted face, then place in front of herself an old photo from the days when her hair was beautiful and combed out and her smile brilliant, the days of her happiness—were my mother ever to compare the two images and ask, Why? Would she not then refuse and protest? Her weakness is no excuse, because despite it she can always put an end to what is an oppressive and insane injustice. Just a smidgen of courage—just a smidgen and the employee refuses to work for a lower salary. The elephant awaits its end. Muhammad Kurayim refuses to save his life by paying a poll tax to his enemies the French and goes to his death calmly, nobly, triumphantly.* The Athenian know-nothings sentence Socrates to death and when on the night of the execution Plato sneaks in to see him, bringing a plan of escape, the teacher hears his enthusiastic pupil out

---

* *Muhammad Kurayim was governor of Alexandria at the time of the French invasion of Egypt in 1798. In resisting the French occupation, he was sentenced to death.*

and refuses to flee and in amazement Plato asks why and Socrates smiles and answers, "Because I have turned my back on this contemptible world."

❖ 10 ❖

The end. I was sitting in the hairdresser's chair. The hairdresser was, as is usually the case, servile, inquisitive, and loquacious. He hated me because I had been visiting his shop for two whole years and he had not yet been able to find out one thing about me. Just my first name. No matter how hard he tried and persisted in trying to drag me into a conversation, I would resist until he gave up in despair and took to cutting my hair in silence. This silence would sometimes be too much for him and he'd talk to the other customers, while I looked down and read. On that particular day, I'd forgotten to bring a book with me to read. I had to read something, so I turned to the magazines arranged on the shelf of the mirror in front of me—back issues of a French magazine called *L'Art du Décor*. I have no interest in decoration, but I picked up an issue and began to leaf through some of the articles dealing with that subject. There were lots of photos of furniture in various styles. I went through the pages fast and exchanged that issue for another. On the first page of the second magazine I saw it—a picture that I stopped at and which attracted me so much that I still remember it clearly. It was a photo of a bedroom in the modern style—a wide low bed close to the ground covered with a black silk sheet. On the wall there was a large painting representing a large solid nose surrounded by numerous intersecting shadows colored in shades that ranged from white to black. The floor of the room was completely covered with white fur and the intersection of the white and the black seemed wonderful. I contemplated the photo and a beautiful and surprising feeling was released inside me that quickly turned into an overwhelming love. Minutes passed as I savored the beauty in the picture. I tried to turn the page and look at another but I couldn't; after a moment I'd go back to my first picture. When I had finished getting my hair cut and was paying, I asked, "Can I keep the magazine?"

He agreed at once and with delight as this presented an opportunity to interfere in my life, bursting into a long prattle about French décor and how elegant it was. It wasn't long before he asked, "Do you want the magazine for the new house, sir? A thousand congratulations, Mr. Isam!"

I freed myself from the hairdresser, tucked the magazine under my arm, and took a taxi home. I was breathless, an adolescent with a photo of a naked woman in his pocket who dashes to his room, locks the door, pulls out the photo panting with desire, and then disappears for hours into a pleasure as overwhelming as if the woman were real. I spent the night smoking hashish and looking at the photo. Every part of it aroused within me a different feeling of beauty—the nose in the middle of the picture, the wrinkled bed covering, the white floor. I drank of beauty until my thirst was quenched and when I lay down on the bed to sleep the light of dawn was filtering in through the openings in the shutters and I knew that I had embarked on a strange, rich experience.

The next day, I left the department and didn't go back to the house. I went to Suleiman Pasha Square, to the big newspaper shop. The vendor smiled showing his gold teeth, pointed to a corner of the shop, and said, "The new foreign magazines are on the right and on the left are the old ones at quarter price."

I paid no attention to the old magazines: the thought of a dust-covered or dog-eared foreign magazine upset me. I stood there for a long time. I leafed through magazines and looked and compared and in the end left after buying two—one French (even though I didn't know French), the other American.

❖ 11 ❖

I spent that night like the one before. Silence, hashish, and dreams. I tried to read a political article in the American magazine but got bored and stopped. It was the pictures alone that attracted me. Everything in the pictures seemed marvelous; even the smallest things had a quiet glamour. A life of exuberance, variety, and resplendence. The streets and the buildings and the people, even the rain and the ice and the beaches. Artists with long beards standing in front of their paintings, musicians dressed all in black sitting at their instruments and sheet music. Even the demonstrations were marvelous—hundreds of people marching in a broad, clean square, their faces white and their hair blond, carrying placards of protest and moving forward in silence; policemen with their strong bodies, elegant uniforms, and shining badges surrounding the demonstration and protecting it. Sometimes a politician would address the demonstrators, in which case he would look dignified and usually be wearing glasses with elegant gold or silver frames. I finished the two magazines and the next day bought more. Day after day, I was totally bewitched. I went overboard, and even though I was so happy with my daily purchases, more than once I caught the newspaper vendor looking at me with doubt and anxiety as I paged through them. It seems he'd noticed that I looked mainly at the pictures, because one day he came up to me and said, "We have a *poster* inside that you'll like. Want to see it?"

I didn't know what *poster* meant, but when I followed him inside I discovered that it was a large colored photo that covered the wall. I counted the money I had with me and it wasn't enough. I didn't buy it but went and borrowed some from my mother and returned and came back to the house bearing four large posters. Huda helped me to cover the four walls of my room with them. I had to pile all my father's paintings in the corner to make space for the posters, and I felt no sorrow or regret. My gloomy room now scintillated with shiny newness. Lying on my bed I could see on the wall a house in the countryside with a pitched roof surrounded by a small garden bordered with a white picket fence and in the far distance a thick forest of tall sesban trees. It was winter; ice covered the ground and on the trees and the roof of the house fragile little snowflakes had fallen.

What was happening to me? I wasn't an adolescent. I was thirty-five. The days of sudden enthusiasms and feverish feelings were gone. My attachment to the foreign pictures was traceable to some idea that I had to sort through and understand. What was it about a picture of a chair or a bed that would send all this joy through me? Was it madness? The insane must have their own logic but we don't know what it is because our contact with them ceases the moment they start behaving in a way different to us. Could insanity be a furious desire like that which had taken hold of me? I pummeled my brains for nights on end until I reached a conclusion, which emerged suddenly and with complete clarity. It wasn't the pictures I liked. What I liked was what the pictures evoked in me. At weddings and on feast days, Egyptian peasant women put on decorated dresses of clashing, garish colors, they dye their hands and feet with henna, and then they hire a cart drawn by a donkey wearing blinkers and spend the day on the cart clapping, ululating, and singing songs. The sight of the women on the cart evokes in me a certain specific, distinctively 'Egyptian' feeling. Equally, the picture of the thick forest covered with snow or the picture of the artist with the pipe and beard evokes in me a feeling of 'the West.' It was the spirit of the West in the pictures that captivated me. That was it exactly. The western spirit surrounds us, we see it in everything, but rarely do we strip it of its outward manifestations. Everything that's elegant about our lives is necessarily western! Examples? The physician's white coat, scientific and even household devices and appliances, a movie star's necktie, a luxury, recent-model car. Everything. Everything we like goes back to them.

When my thinking got to this point of clarity, I was afraid I'd forget what I'd understood, or that less important thoughts would obliterate it later, so I got an exercise book out of my desk and wrote on the first page, "I have just realized that I have fallen captive to the spirit of the West, for the more certain I become of how useless we are, the more their spirit appears to me to be running over with amazing potential."

❖ 12 ❖

The mystery of my passion now solved, my infatuation with the pictures inevitably began to fade. The pictures were merely my path to the Beloved and there were many other paths that would bring me closer. Why shouldn't I live this spirit of theirs instead of searching for it in pictures—experience it, breathe it, and touch it? I would travel to their countries, to their sun and their ice and their buildings and their faces. And if I was incapable of traveling, I would look for them here in Egypt. They came here and roamed the streets and previously I had seen them a lot and paid them no attention. It was amazing that you could see beauty dozens of times and pass it by without being affected; then one day, in a moment of divine inspiration, you would discover it and your body would tremble with burning ecstasy.

I would spend the days in the department daydreaming and anxious. I didn't read and I didn't look at anyone. I would see my loved ones in my mind's eye and burn with longing to meet them. As soon as the time to leave came, I would rush off to them. I would go to their places—the Pyramids, the Egyptian Museum, Saladin's Citadel. Everyday I would meet them somewhere new. I would pretend to be looking, like them, at the place, while following them with my eyes. I devoured them and memorized their details in my mind—their faces and bodies, their laughter and voices. Then I would chew over these with pleasure each night as I smoked hashish. Sometimes I would ask, "Doesn't God realize that they are His most exquisite creatures? Can God be bent on torturing them the way He will torture us? Even their adulterous women, their thieves, and their murderers—will God punish them by grilling their beautiful white skins? It's not possible. God could not have created such splendor only to burn it later on." One night I stood in front of the mirror and looked at my coarse hair and my ugly dark face. I thought of the faces of my mother, my father, and all those whom I knew. I was disgusted and rushed to write down in my notebook, "We deserve torture because we are disfigured."

Sometimes I would borrow money from my mother and sometimes I would steal from her purse. With it I bought smart new clothes that I would wear every day, and I would buy a pack of imported cigarettes and go to them, at food festivals, culture centers, classical music concerts—any place I knew they would be I went to and with time I developed a lover's experience. I found out that Italian pizza was crisp and thin and American thick and stuffed. With a single glance I could distinguish the uprightness of the Germans, the delicacy of the French, the vivacity of the Italians, and the natural transparency and simplicity of the Americans; all these beautiful variations, like gorgeous colors, seemed to be separate, but blended in the end to produce light. The poles of love and knowledge met and the circle was completed, thus qualifying me to take a new step upward that would bring me closer to the melting point of ecstasy.

❖ 13 ❖

The German Cultural Center is a small elegant building on a noisy street. There was a photographic exhibition. The photographer was standing there receiving the visitors—a young German man in his early twenties with a small pointed beard, blue eyes, and long hair like a girl's which he tied in a tress that hung down his back. He shook my hand, smiled in welcome, mumbled some English words in a low voice, and I went in. The visitors were Germans and Egyptians. The Germans wore jeans and T-shirts and the Egyptians were smartly dressed.

Expensive scents mixed and luxurious new clothes scintillated. I detached myself from the flow of the crowd and started the exhibition from the end, viewing the photos on my own. Some had been taken in Munich, the photographer's hometown, but most were taken in Egypt. There was everything that would please the tourist—a cart laden with limes, a liquorice drink vendor clapping his little cymbals, and another of a man wearing a turban buying a watermelon and having the vendor cut it open in front of him to prove it was ripe. I stopped in front of a picture of a number of young boys in el-Husayn Square, their bodies emaciated and their faces worn with weakness and malnutrition. They were standing barefoot in torn gallabiyas and laughing before the camera and one of them had pulled his gallabiya up to the top of his legs and was sticking his backside out in an obscene movement.

"That photo is an insult to Egypt, wouldn't you agree?"

The voice came from behind me. Clear English and a friendly tone. I turned and saw her.

You are walking in the street on an ordinary day on your way to some ordinary event; the cameras take you by surprise and the passersby rush up to shake your hand and congratulate you, all because you've won a huge prize just by virtue of being the first to cross the street that morning—that was the sort of surprise I felt when I saw her. Deep blue eyes that once you had caught sight of you could not pass by as one might dozens of other faces. I was drawn into them and the rest of her beautiful face disappeared into the background. Eyes from which there was no escape. I looked at them and stammered. Then I said in a deep voice to hide my agitation, "Why? I can't see anything insulting to Egypt in this picture."

She came closer and her smile widened. She radiated beauty. She said, "I know lots of beautiful things in Egypt that deserve to be photographed more than barefoot children."

By now I could distinguish a small nose, plump rosy lips, and smooth long yellow hair that she wore straight and that fell below her shoulders. The body was full and ripe, and, restraining myself from looking at her delicious, ample breasts, I said, "If you don't take photographs of the barefoot children, the poor, and the piles of garbage in Egypt, then what are you going to take photographs of? The Pyramids and the Sphinx?"

I was being sarcastic and my voice dripped bitterness. She asked me in amazement, "Are you Egyptian?"

"I am. Unfortunately."

Her surprise increased and she said nothing. I turned back to the picture, then passed on to the next one and stood looking at it, my heart beating. It pounded when I heard her steps behind me. I became aware of her at my side, and heard her voice again, saying, "How strange you should feel sorry because you're Egyptian. Since I was a child, I've longed to be Egyptian."

Her face flushed a little and a dreamy look passed over her eyes. I laughed and said, "What country are you from?"

"I'm German, but I love Egypt. I love it passionately."

"You love Egypt in exactly the way you'd love an exotic show at the circus, or rare animals at the zoo. But believe me, if you'd been born Egyptian it would have been a tragedy."

The conversation had to be extended. She stated her surprise at my opinion and said that she had spent two years in Egypt during which she'd gotten to know dozens of Egyptians but she'd never heard anyone express this point of

view before. I rushed on, heatedly confirming my opinion
while she continued to listen. The astonishment and disbelief
in her face drove me to even greater obstinacy. I stated to her
that Egypt was a dead country and that civilizations were
like any other being that passes through the stages of baby-
hood, childhood, and youth and then grows old and dies,
and that our civilization had died hundreds of years ago, so
there was no hope of reviving it. I told her that the Egyptians
had the mentality of servants and slaves and understood no
language but that of the stick, and I told her the story of the
poet al-Mutanabbi when he came to Egypt, translating for
her the lines that go "Buy not the slave without his stick!/
Filthy and ill-starred indeed is the slave!"*

We became completely engrossed in our conversation
and stopped bothering with the photos. Nor did we notice
the time, and in the end we found ourselves making our way,
still talking, to the exit. She stopped and gave me a deep,
friendly look that pierced my heart, and said, smiling as
always, "Really, I thank you for this enjoyable conversation.
I'm happy to have got to know the opinion of an Egyptian
intellectual on his country. True, I don't agree with your
opinion, but I respect it because it is authentic."

Then she laughed and went on, "Just imagine! I still
haven't learned your name."

I laughed wholeheartedly as she tried, haltingly, to pronounce my name, and then asked her hers and she replied,
"My name is Jutta."

---

* *Abu al-Tayyib Ahmad ibn Husayn al-Mutanabbi (915–965) is regarded as one of the
greatest poets in the Arabic language.*

As she pronounced the name, her lips formed a delicious rosy circle. Then she shrugged her shoulders and said, "Just a German name. Do you like it?"

I nodded my head and she held out her hand to shake mine, saying in farewell, "Isam. Happy to have met you. I hope we get a chance to continue this discussion some other time."

Then she turned to leave but I called out suddenly, "Where are you going now?

"Now?"

She appeared to be thinking about what lay behind the question and then answered slowly, "I don't have anything particular to do."

"Let's continue our conversation then, somewhere else. I'm inviting you. Do you have any objection?"

She looked at me seriously for a moment, then nodded her head, and after a few minutes we were getting into a taxi. I hesitated a little, then said to the driver, "Hotel Sémiramis."

❖ 14 ❖

I am neither brave nor an expert in women, and when I think now of what I did with Jutta I am amazed at my audacity; it feels to me as though the person who did it was someone else, that someone daring and capable had slipped inside me and stayed there pushing me. I resisted, but he overcame my weakness and gave me strength. When a fire breaks out or someone comes close to drowning or some incredible event occurs, a person who is completely insignificant in ordinary life may be transformed in an instant into an extraordinary being and resolutely undertake acts that nobody, including himself, would have imagined he had it in him to perform. I

73

asked Jutta to go with me? Me, the broken-spirited, whom a glance from a doorkeeper would throw into confusion and who didn't dare to direct a look—not even a look—at the face of a beautiful woman! I sat next to her in the taxi watching her. She had folded her arms and turned to look at the street from the window. She was wearing a blue denim jacket with a black top beneath it that revealed her white upper chest and neck, wide pants of a light white material, and, on her small feet, simple black shoes. She had washed her hair but not combed it, so that its dark thickets intertwined in thick tresses. I caught the driver watching through the car mirror and smiling, the only way to explain my relationship with Jutta in his mind being my sexual prowess. That was the most a servant like him could comprehend. I felt a sudden rage against the driver but suppressed it and asked her, "What are you doing in Egypt?"

She answered with a laugh, "Uh! That's a long story. I came to Egypt as part of a tourist group and fell in love with it so much that it ruined the rest of my life. When I went back to Germany, everything seemed to me deathly boring so I made up my mind to come and live in Egypt and here I am."

"Do you have a job?"

"Yes. An Egyptian friend pulled some strings to get me a job as a secretary in an import-export company. I get a generous salary, but every six months, I have to pay a huge amount in dollars to renew my residency."

I must have been silent for a little because she suddenly laughed and asked me, "Does my story sound strange?"

After a moment's hesitation, I said, "Yes."

The hotel was crowded—a lofty ceiling, huge expensive complicated dangling chandeliers, corridors and lights and servants dressed all in black. As I crossed the entryway with Jutta, she asked me if I knew the hotel and I answered that I didn't, so she nodded and led me up the marble stairway to the bar. It seemed she knew the place well. A smartly dressed waiter received us and led us to a table on the terrace that looks out over the Nile. Jutta asked me gaily, "Would it annoy you if I ordered alcohol?"

"It would annoy me if you ordered anything else," I replied.

When she laughed, her lips revealed small, regular, shining white teeth. The waiter brought a bottle of beer for me and a glass of gin for Jutta. I suddenly got worried when I thought of how much money I had on me, but then I relaxed at the thought that it would cover, at the least, a beer for me and another drink for her. On the other shore, the lights were shimmering in the distance and a cool evening breeze was pushing at the surface of the water and breaking it up into waves that made a low murmuring sound. Jutta drank from her glass and looked at the night, seemingly intoxicated by her surroundings. Then she asked me, in a tone fluctuating between reproach and playfulness, "Can anyone hate a country as beautiful as this?"

"Trust me, nature in Germany is no less beautiful, but to you it's familiar and everything familiar loses its beauty."

"That's not true, because after two years here the sight of the Nile still bewitches me—more so perhaps than at the beginning. And you have to remember too that what I like about Egypt isn't just its views."

"What else do you like?" I asked her sarcastically, being now a little drunk.

"The people have extremely warm and kind feelings."

I laughed so loudly that a lady at the next table turned and looked at me. Jutta asked me, "What's so funny?"

"Your opinion of Egyptians. Exactly what 'kind feelings' are you talking about? Egyptians are merely poisonous insects. That is the scientific description for them."

"But I've never noticed that."

"Of course, you couldn't possibly notice it because you're foreign and a woman and beautiful! Listen. Would it be correct for us to consider this waiter a kind man just because he treats us politely? The courtesy he shows to customers is imposed upon him by circumstances stronger than himself. If you want to know what he's really like, ask one of his neighbors or his family."

She rested her chin on her hands and looked at me for a moment. Then she said, "Your way of talking is crude and your vision is crude, but it pleases me somehow."

I ordered another drink for her and a beer and felt a strong desire to talk, to tell. I was afraid Jutta would get bored and felt embarrassed to be baring my soul in front of her, but once the alcohol had started to have its effect, a fervor rose within me that made me speak with a wild enthusiasm. I told her about my father and mother and the Chemistry Authority. I even spoke about Huda the maid, and Jutta kept listening to me with interest. Sometimes she would stop me to ask a question about some detail or other and sometimes I was so bitter I would burst into laughter, but on these occasions she would not share my laughter. She would just look at me with her deep eyes and I would feel that she understood me. When I finished, the bar had almost emptied and Jutta said slowly, looking at her glass and turning it between the palms of her hands, "Isam. I don't want to make any comments on what you said. I'm afraid anything I say would sound foolish or childish. But I'm thinking now of Frederick, a German friend, who was the first person who told me about Egypt. He's an engineer and he spent ten years in Egypt. Do you know what he told me once? He said that he'd visited most of the countries in the world and he'd never seen a country as full of talented people as Egypt and that he felt sorry that the talented people in Egypt faced such great problems."

She said this looking at me and slowly nodding her head as though to emphasize the meaning, and it occurred to me at that moment that her face seemed to me to have two different forms: sometimes it would be delicate and dreamy, and then it looked like that of a wonderful gay little girl, and sometimes her features changed and a severe cast would cover it.

"Let's have another drink," I said and she replied gently, "I'm sorry. It's late and I have to be going."

When I looked over the check, my disquiet must have shown because she brought her head close and whispered, "I can share it with you."

I thanked her and refused and paid the check, leaving the waiter a big tip, and we got up and descended the stairs in silence. There was an insistent question suspended between us and I felt she was aware of what was going on in my head because, as soon as we went out on to the street, she immediately took the initiative and extended her hand to shake mine, saying, "Thank you so much. I had a good time. I hope we can meet again. Do you have a telephone at home?"

I looked at her for a moment. Then I said suddenly and in an unequivocal tone, "I shall never leave you."

She laughed and asked, "What do you mean?"

"You know what I mean. I am incapable of leaving you. I want to be with you."

Once again, my audacity amazed me. Jutta looked at me as though sizing me up and her face shifted into its serious mode. Then she said, giving weight to each word, "Isam. Listen. It's true that I like you and find you very interesting. I'd even be okay with your coming home with me. But that would cause me problems I can do without."

"What problems?" I asked. She sighed and replied, "Before I came to Egypt, Frederick warned me, because Egyptians have their own different traditions. You know what I mean, of course. But I ignored the warning. I didn't take him seriously. And one night I tried to invite a male friend to my apartment, and that made Mr. Shaaban very mad and almost caused a scandal."

"And who's this Mr. Shaaban?"

"Shaaban the grocer. His shop is below my building and he stays up until midnight. I don't want to make trouble with him. He's a religious zealot and can't accept my bringing a man to my apartment. That's what he told me clearly the first time."

I found myself yelling in fury, "Are you going to let the grocer control your private life?"

"Please understand. I don't want to hurt his feelings and I also know that challenging tradition in Egypt leads to disaster. Frederick made that very clear to me."

My fury reached its peak and I was silent for a moment. Then I suddenly found myself taking hold of her and pulling her along with me while she shouted, "Isam! Wait, please! I'm serious."

I paid no attention to her yelling and pulled her along until I'd got her into a taxi that was waiting in front of the hotel. Then I sat down beside her and whispered imperiously in her ear, "Tell the driver your address."

She looked at me hesitantly, then said to the driver in broken Arabic, "Madinet Nasr, Abbas el-Aqqad Street."

On the way to her house we talked, but a slight anxiety made the conversation a little tense, so it came to a stop. I was not afraid. I could feel a sweeping, driving strength flowing through my limbs. No doubt it was the alcohol, but I had grasped that I was living the most important moments of my life and that I had to take them in my hands or they would be lost for ever. I was ready to confront Shaaban. If he objected to my going upstairs with Jutta, I would hit him. I would take anything heavy from his shop and hit him hard on the head. It didn't matter to me whether I killed him; I would not let Jutta slip away from me and I would never allow anyone to keep me away from her. Who was this Shaaban? A grocer with religion! Someone who would cheat and swindle his customers and pray each prayer on the dot. Base, stupid, parasitical, and spiteful, like any Egyptian. I would address him in the language he understood—*Buy not the slave without his stick*, as al-Mutanabbi said. Jutta decided to have the taxi stop some way before her house and after we got out and the taxi had left, she whispered anxiously, casting a look toward the house, "Shaaban's shop is open. There's going to be trouble."

I pulled her by the hand and as we went toward the house I said confidently, "When we get to the entrance of the building, you go on ahead and leave me to deal with him."

The shop was small and bore the name *Faith Grocery*. A fat bearded man wearing a white gallabiya was picking things up and dragging cans and barrels inside. Shaaban was getting ready to close. From his appearance as I approached with Jutta, it seemed to me that he was fierce and that the battle would not be easy. We reached the entrance and Jutta went inside quickly while I slowed down in front of the shop. I stopped and turned to Shaaban, who left the cans and came up to me, looking at me warily. I stared at him in fury, and then shouted in a loud voice, "As-Salamu alaykum!"*

He didn't reply, but kept looking at me in silence, combing his beard with his fingers and weighing up the situation before intervening. His eyes were narrow and treacherous and his brow was broad, with a dark round prayer spot splattered on it. Was this the face of a Believer? How pleased with himself he looked! No doubt he was confident he had won his Lord's favor in full. I hate animals like that. Ignorant and base and arrogant. I approached until I was standing right in front of him. The small distance that lay between us brought his face within striking distance. I fixed my eyes on his and yelled in the voice of someone who wants to start a quarrel, "I said, As-Salamu alaykum!"

For a moment he didn't seem to understand. Perhaps it was the suddenness of my appearance or he could smell the smell of alcohol on my breath, but suddenly he lowered his gaze and muttered as he turned around and went back

---

* As-salamu alaykum *('Peace be upon you')* is the approved Islamic greeting, to *which any Muslim is expected to respond* Wa-alaykum as-salam wa-rahmat Allahi wa-barakatuh *('And upon you peace and the mercy of God and His blessings').*

to his original position, "Wa-alaykum as-salam wa rahmat Allah. Welcome."

Shaaban was broken and went back to his cans but I watched him closely for a moment until I was sure he had resumed his work as though nothing had happened. Then I walked away from him slowly so he wouldn't think I was weak and return to the fray. Each step that brought me closer to the entrance to the building was like treading on his stupid huge head. Jutta was waiting in the entrance. She looked happy and asked me gaily as we mounted the stairs to her apartment, "What did you do to him? Didn't he try to stop you?"

Proudly I answered, as though what had happened was a trivial matter, "I treated him the way an Egyptian ought to be treated."

The door opened and the apartment received us with a smell of damp. Jutta put out her hand and turned on the light. There was a large reception room, a kitchen, a bathroom, and an inner room separated from the reception room by a long corridor. The furniture—as is usually the case with furnished apartments—looked old, used, and noticeably pieced together, as though it were a mediocre set for some play. I sat on a long red couch with a table in front of me on which I saw scattered papers, banknotes, coins, and a German magazine, which was open. Jutta smiled and said in a voice that showed that from now on she would be feeling like a hostess, "I don't have anything to drink except two bottles of red wine. What do you say?"

"Great."

She went into the kitchen, then returned after a few minutes with a tray on which were a bottle of wine and two

81

glasses. As she poured me a glass, she said, "Red wine is supposed to be drunk warm but I prefer it cold. I hope you don't mind?"

"It's fine," I said as I sipped from my glass and watched her. As she poured the wine, her long blonde hair falling in front of her eyes so that she had to raise it with the side of her wonderful, delicate hand, she looked as though she were part of a rosy dream too beautiful for anyone to believe. The wine had a delicious bite to it. Jutta asked me, her face serious again, "Do you expect Shaaban will call the police?"

"What?"

She burst out laughing, then smiled apologetically and said, "Don't think I'm weak. I'm not a coward, but I don't like problems and I know what fanatics are like. They're all the same. We have fanatics like Shaaban in Germany too."

"Do you mind if we forget about Shaaban completely?" I asked her with a smile and she answered with a nod and then immediately said gaily, "You know, Isam, our meeting tonight is one of the strangest things that's happened to me in my life."

She laughed and I said nothing, so she went on, resting her back against the chair, "I'm not 'a good girl' in the normal sense of the words. I often get involved in relationships just because I'm feeling bored or because some man attracts me in some particular situation. These are what we call one-night stands. All the same, this is the first time I've jumped into bed with a man so fast. Just think, a few hours ago we didn't know one another and now here you are spending the night in my apartment, and I feel as if I've known you for ages."

The wine had expelled any remaining fear and I got up, went over to her, took her hand, kissed it, and leaned my face against hers. She, however, drew away, laughing, and said, "No. Not that fast. It would be too comic if we went through the door of the apartment straight into the bedroom."

I sat down, poured myself another glass, and thought that what was happening was so beautiful that I wanted to stretch it out so as to savor every detail. I always rush to the climax, and when I reach it, it burns brightly and then is extinguished and all that's left is a distant warm memory. Then I am overcome with melancholy and I blame myself for making so much haste to get through the pleasure, when I could have nurtured it at length in my hands.

"Are you aware that your appearance is deceiving?" she said.

"In what way?"

"At first I thought you were shy and had no daring, but then I discovered you were the opposite."

"Your first impression was correct. My behavior tonight amazes me. In fact, I'm a weak person and usually incapable of confrontation."

"I can't believe that."

"At least, that's the person I was a few hours ago."

Smiling and drawing close to me with a flushed face, she said, "What do you mean?"

"I mean that I behaved bravely tonight because I was with you."

She came closer and whispered, "I love your words."

I kissed her and then she drew her head back and said, "I'm feeling lazy. Will you get up and fetch the other bottle of wine?"

I kissed her as I rose. I felt the texture of her cheek as it gave under my lip and I covered her with kisses as she submitted to my embrace. Then she smiled, stretched out her arms, and said, "See what you've done to me?"

The skin of her arms was all goose bumps.

I said, "What does that mean?" and she laughed and said, "It means something extremely important."

I kissed her again, no longer capable of making out what my eyes were seeing. I buried my nose in her hair, everything dissolving into a magical beauty, and she whispered to me, laughing, "What do you say we make an agreement? You fetch the bottle from the kitchen and I'll go ahead of you to the bedroom."

❖

The light of three candles flickered in the darkness of the room. The dark and the light mixed with the taste of the wine, the heat, and a calm, good smell that emanated from her body, and I gathered her to me, my feelings expanding, their roots digging in as I returned to a real moment that I had known once, long ago, then lost, and to which I had now returned. I wished I could whisper to her what I was experiencing, that I could contain her with my feelings as I contained her with my body. A magical dream extricated me from the familiar ugly reality that was forever crushing me in its unforgiving grip.

She told me, "I'm feeling sleepy."

Then she moved close and whispered, "I'd like you to hold me in your arms until morning."

I watched the stillness of sleep flow little by little into her tranquil face.

❖

I had been certain that you would arise like the sun and had waited for you. I had told them about you and no one had believed me, but I had suffered and never lost hope. I believed in you. I believed that some time you would suddenly appear in all your glory, come to cure me with your hands of the wounds of cruelty and to melt the darkness with your smile. When that happened, all that would remain of the loneliness, impotence, and pain would be the terrible rending memories. I would gather you to me and empty these into your breast until I was calm, and then sleep.

In the darkness my face contracted. A shudder ran through me and I surrendered myself to weeping. My tears wet her face and she awoke, stretched out her hand, lit a lamp over the bed, gazed into my face, and asked me with concern, "Are you crying?"

I didn't answer and she said nothing for a moment, as though she understood. Then she looked at the clock and said, "Six! I have to get up now! I'm supposed to be in my office in an hour."

She got up naked and went to the window and opened it, and the room was bathed in daylight, a cool breeze stealing in. She glanced at her face in the mirror and asked me as she left the room, "Tea or coffee with breakfast?"

As I was sipping my coffee, I asked her, "Shall I see you tonight?"

"If you really want to."

I smiled and made no comment.

"You can pick me up at the office after work. I leave at three."

When we left the house, Shaaban's shop was closed and the road was completely empty. She said to me, "Won't you come with me to see where I work? It's close by, at the end of the street."

I walked next to her for some minutes until she stopped in front of a small two-story house. On the balcony of the first floor I saw a large sign that said "Mustafa Yusri. Import-Export." Jutta pointed to the sign and said, "This is where I work. It's the first floor, apartment 3."

She looked around, bent quickly over my face, kissed me, and whispered, "I'll see you at three."

Then she went into the building.

I walked alone until I reached the main street, where I stopped a taxi. The traces of sleep were still on the driver's face. I looked out of the window. Life was stirring in the street. People were gathering as they do every morning at the bus stops, starting a new day with faces still exhausted from the one before. It seemed strange to me that nothing was different that morning. I'd expected that everything I saw would appear to me in a new, wonderful shape, but everything was just as it had been and it was as if I'd never met Jutta or lived with her the most beautiful moments of my life, as if a new man had not been born within me.

The moment I opened the door of the house, my mother met me with cries and tears, "My heart and the Lord will be angry with you until the Day of Resurrection."

I ignored her and turned my steps in silence toward my room but she caught up with me in the corridor, grabbed me by the hand, and said, "Is this any way to treat me, Isam? Shouldn't you be ashamed of yourself? You don't mind leaving me worrying about you the whole night? Don't you know I'm sick and my health can't take any anxiety?"

All she cared about was the effect of the anxiety on her health. I looked at her. I stared into her eyes until the details vanished and my vision clouded over. This went on for a few moments. When I came to myself, I made my way with exhausted steps to my room while my mother continued to bewail her bad luck in a tearful voice. I knew I wouldn't be able to sleep so I didn't try for long. I opened the window and the sun's rays spread through the room. Huda brought me the newspapers and coffee. My eyes scanned the headlines and I threw them aside. My powers of concentration were destroyed. I would wait until three and that was all I was capable of thinking about. At three I would meet her. I would kiss her and hold her and she would sleep in my arms as she had done yesterday. The time passed like an eon and when it was almost two o'clock I got up, washed, and put on my clothes. My mother caught sight of me and rushed after me fearfully, asking, "Are you going out?"

I muttered yes without turning so she grabbed my arm and said, "Don't, Isam, I beg you. You haven't slept and your nerves are tired."

I released my arm from her grip by force and left, the door slamming behind me.

It was hot and the sweat was pouring off my forehead. As I waited for the streetcar in the middle of the crowd, I was thinking that I'd be saving the cost of a taxi. There was still an hour to go and I would undoubtedly need money that night. After half an hour the streetcar came and it was crowded. I pushed my way so far in among the other passengers that their bodies hid me from the light and darkness reigned about me. I reached Madinet Nasr station and pulled out of my pocket the piece of paper on which I'd written down Jutta's address in case I forgot. I walked for ten minutes to get to the office.

It got so hot that I removed my jacket and undid the buttons of my shirt. The house looked as it had that morning, with the same sign saying "Yusri Mustafa. Import-Export." This time I hoped that the doorkeeper would stop me as I crossed the entrance to the building. As of yesterday, I had become a strong master. I would repel him confidently and powerfully. No one tried to stop me and when I entered the office my heart was beating hard. I would see Jutta now. Should I rush up to her, embrace her, and cover her face with kisses in front of her colleagues? I put off thinking about that. The office opposite the door was empty. A pack of cigarettes and an open newspaper indicated that the employee who sat there had left on some errand and would be coming back. In the corner of the room was a young girl with her hair covered; she was typing. I stood for a minute in front of the empty desk, then turned toward where the girl was sitting. She stopped typing and raised her face to me. She was beautiful but the way she looked at me was empty of any expression, as though she did not know me and did not welcome me but, at the same time, my presence neither surprised nor bothered her. If she hadn't returned my greeting with a slight nod of the head, I would have thought that she hadn't seen me.

"May I see Miss Jutta, please?"

"Who?"

"Miss Jutta, the German lady."

The girl smiled. Later, when I thought over that smile, I understood everything.

"There's nobody by that name working here."

"No. She does work here, I'm certain. I have an appointment with her. Please be so kind as to tell her that Isam is waiting for her."

This time she didn't turn toward me. She went on striking the keys with her hands. Her indifference to my presence annoyed me so I went up to her and shouted, "You, Miss! Can't you hear? I'm telling you to inform Jutta that I'm here."

She raised her head and looked at me in silence. Then she resumed her typing. I lost all control of my nerves. I started shouting and was soon insulting her and then I shoved her on the shoulder. I felt the solidity of her shoulder bone against my hand. With the noise, a few employees emerged and a thin, bald man of about forty wearing a smart gray suit and with wide, powerful eyes came toward me. He took hold of my arm and asked me roughly what I wanted. I answered him that I wanted to see Jutta, and when he replied as had the girl with the covered hair, I exploded in his face. All he did was to tighten his grip on my wrist until it hurt so much I was completely paralyzed. I started shouting and cursing them all and in my ears cries of 'crazy' and 'police' mixed with one another and I found myself being dragged by the man in the gray suit toward the door. Then he gave me a powerful push on my back with his hands that expelled me from the apartment.

I staggered and almost fell on the stairs and he quickly and violently closed the door to the office.

I rushed down the stairs and into the street as fast as I could. I didn't feel anger or surprise. I was like someone who wants at the last moment to prevent a certain disaster. I started running down the street. Out of the corner of my eye, I could see the passersby stopping and staring in amazement. After a few minutes, I reached Jutta's house. I stopped for a moment in front of it. I was panting and copious sweat was flowing over my face and neck. I started to cross the entrance when a deep voice took me by surprise.

"Where do you think you're going, buddy?"

His tone was impertinent and it occurred to me as I turned to face him that it must be Shaaban, Shaaban with his beard and the dark spot on his forehead and his baseness, Shaaban whose coarse skin oozed grease and malevolence. I rushed toward him and fell on him with a blow to the face that connected perfectly, making his huge body stagger. Before he could stand straight, I got in another quick blow and kicked him hard in the belly, then pushed him so that he fell to the ground. I threw myself upon him and proceeded to beat him on the head until I felt the stickiness of blood on my fingers.

❖

The plot was well laid, and when I now review these events and details in tranquility, I am possessed by admiration for their skill and careful planning.

Truly, they'd set things up perfectly. At the investigation, Shaaban said that he didn't know me and that there was no preexisting hostility between us. He said he had seen me going into the building the previous night but had been afraid to question me as he had realized that I was under the influence of alcohol and was afraid I might harm him. He denied emphatically—as did the residents, owner, and door-keeper of the building—that a German girl lived there. Similarly, Yusri Mustafa (the owner of the office and the bald man with the gray suit) accused me in his deposition to the investigation of being insane and denied that any German girl had ever worked in his office. Even the waiter from the Semiramis bar, when summoned by the police, said that I had spent the evening in the bar the previous day and that I had drunk a lot but denied that a foreign girl had been with me. He emphasized that I had arrived alone and left alone, at half-past one in the morning. When the investigator asked him if he had noticed anything abnormal about me, he replied that he had noticed that I was talking to myself in English in a loud voice and laughing but that at the time he had considered the matter quite normal, attributing it to my extreme drunkenness.

❖ 15 ❖

The circle closed tight around me. There wasn't a single gap through which I could escape. All of them—all of those who knew my worth and were infuriated by my superiority—conspired against me. Everyone who hated me and whom I despised, Dr. Sa'id and Shaaban and the waiter, even my mother and Huda and my aged grandmother—all of them had united to prevent a recognized danger that would have crushed them had I become united with Jutta, I who had drawn close and seen. They conspired and succeeded and then they isolated me in a special place, dressed me in special clothes, and tightened their grip upon me, and I could find no alternative to surrender, at which point they pretended to be sorry for me, and now they visit me and bring me roses and boxes of chocolate. They talk to the doctor about me and draw expressions of anxiety and pleading on their faces, then tell me goodbye with a glance that reassures them that I will never be able to slip from their clutches, and leave.

The Kitchen Boy

FOR SOME UNKNOWN REASON, intelligence is associated in people's minds with brightness of eye, and anyone who wants to prove he's brilliant stares into others' faces, focusing on their eyes. This way, they may witness for themselves how brightly his own flash and the inordinate acumen with which they shine. Hisham's eyes, on the other hand, did not shine at all, and were small too. Similarly his brown complexion, unremarkable features, meager body, and natural tendency toward shyness and introspection made him appear simply one of those undifferentiated thousands who throng the streets and buses. As soon as Hisham began to speak, however, you would be amazed, because he would grasp what you were saying immediately and comment on it before you'd finished. Then he'd fall silent and quietly smile, as though apologizing for having left you behind. They say—though God knows how true this is—that Hisham learned to speak very early and that before he was three years old he knew how to wind the old Grundig tape reel, put it in place on the machine, thread it, and finally press the button to make the music come out. Because Hisham and I were at the same secondary school, I myself had the opportunity to observe his talents, which carried everything before them. Hisham wasn't one of those who would plod away at his studies for hours and hours; he would understand the lesson in class and read it once at home, after which he might do a few exercises. Then he would effortlessly achieve the highest marks. In math, he'd often stand up and explain to us, in his quiet voice, how he had solved a problem that had defeated us all, and when he had finished and the teacher had thanked him, we would stare at him, in admiration or with envy. He, however, hated being the object of attention, so he'd busy himself by searching for his pencil, or lean back and start a conversation with the student sitting behind him. Hisham came first in the school in the Secondary General exam. He wanted to go into engineering but his mother wept and pleaded with him in the name of his dead father, reminding him that he was her only child and that all her hopes were pinned on his becoming a doctor, and Hisham submitted and spent five years studying medicine, during which he maintained the highest marks. They say that his grasp of the material at his oral exam extracted the grudging admiration of even the grimmest and most savage of the examiners, and they also say that after Dr. Mandour, the celebrated professor of anatomy, had finished examining Hisham, he stood up, went over to him, shook his hand, and ordered him a cold drink (a gesture of respect rarely granted anyone by the great professor). Because Hisham was so outstanding (but also because he wasn't the son of a professor at the university or a relative of a minister), he placed twentieth in his class on graduating.

Hisham was appointed a resident in General Surgery, an outcome with which he was genuinely pleased. When his mother got the news (she was peeling potatoes in front of the television at the time), she was thrilled and gave whoops of joy, then wept, blessed the Lord, and performed two prayer prostrations in thanks to Him. She quickly spread the news by telephone to relatives and friends, got dressed, and went out to buy sherbet and pastries. When the first people, some neighbors, arrived to offer their congratulations, his mother (who had now assumed the grave and dignified air befitting the mother of a surgeon) related to them how Hisham hadn't made any effort to win the appointment; on the contrary, it was they who had insisted on appointing him, in view of his excellence. And on the second day, when more well-wishers came, the mother recounted a whole dialogue that had taken place between the chairman of the surgery department and her son in which the former had urged Hisham to agree to work with him, while Hisham had asked for a chance to think it over, as he wasn't quite sure.

◈

Hisham knocked on the door, opened it a little, politely, and advanced a very short distance into the room. Dr. Bassiouni, the chairman of the department, was sitting talking with three members of the teaching staff. When Hisham appeared, they paused and looked at him attentively, and he felt his heart beating hard. He took a deep breath, smiled in a politely friendly way, and said, "Good morning."

They didn't answer but went on looking. Having to explain his presence, he said, "Hisham Fakhri, the new resident, sir."

"Wait outside," was the chairman's perfunctory response, after which he resumed his conversation with the professors. Hisham left and started pacing the hall. He smoked three cigarettes. When the professors emerged from the chairman's office, he repeated everything he had done the time before, starting with knocking on the door and introducing himself, since Dr. Bassiouni had, in the few minutes that had elapsed, completely forgotten about him.

"Listen, my boy. Do you know what your job in the department here is?"

Hisham was at a loss for a reply.

"Your job here is that of the kitchen boy," said the chairman, breaking out into quick, repeated bursts of laughter and playing with his long sideburns. Hisham was on the verge of laughing too, out of politeness, but fortunately an inner voice warned him against doing so.

"Do you know what the kitchen boy is, in the kitchen? He's the boy who collects the onion peelings and washes down the tiles and gets it in the neck from the cooks. There you have it: the resident in surgery is precisely the kitchen boy in the kitchen."

Hisham nodded. The chairman continued, "You will do what we tell you to do. Be careful not to object or complain. Everything has its price. You want to become a surgeon? Then you have to pay the price, just as we all did—in sweat and toil, abuse and insults. And three years from now, if I like you, I will sign with this very hand the decision appointing you an assistant lecturer at the university. If, on the other hand, I do not like you, I will dispense with your services and you will go back to the Ministry of Health to do donkey work, just like the rest of the donkeys there."

At this point it seemed to occur to the chairman that Hisham had taken up too much of his time and he glowered, and shouted at him in a sudden fury, "Enough! On your way! Go do the paperwork with personnel!"

❖

Dr. Bassiouni is too well known to require introduction. He is Chairman of the Department of General Surgery and likewise of the Arab Surgeons Association, and member of dozens of international medical associations. In addition to all this he is a public figure whose views on the economy are published in the newspapers and who is invited to appear on television during Ramadan to tell us about his favorite dishes. And Dr. Bassiouni is above all—and let us not forget this— an exceptional surgeon, who has made his incontestable mark in the annals of surgery. Being all of this, he is, naturally, different from you and me—we the lusterless ordinary people, devoid of any value or talent. The fact is that Dr. Bassiouni is as odd as he is exceptional and skilled and his strange ways attract curiosity and comment, not to mention fear and admiration. In the August heat, for example, Dr. Bassiouni will wear a short-sleeved shirt like any other citizen, but—inevitably—he will wear around his neck a tie so long that it reaches to below his belt. No one knows why he insists on the tie when he is not wearing a jacket. Nor does anyone know what the point is of this tie being so long. In addition, he chooses clothes of bright clashing colors that he seems to have chosen deliberately to not match (though they say that he acquired this practice during his stay in America). And while it is accepted that one should let his sideburns grow a little, Dr. Bassiouni has gone to excessive lengths in this respect, draping his face with long gray sideburns that extend from below his ears and give him the appearance of a nineteenth-century English lord, or a Greek grocer from Alexandria. Despite which, his general appearance, with his sideburns, flashy colors, small bald patch, short, stout body, and rapid, irritable movements is not without good looks and certainly gives no hint of his sixty years.

Dr. Bassiouni has never gotten married, a fact which, according to one interpretation, is attributable to his faithfulness to an old love that ended painfully. On the administrative side, it is well known that the doctor's department is one of the best organized at el-Qasr el-Aini Hospital, and this is true even though the doctor—with the exception of operating days—spends less than an hour there each day, after which he leaves in a hurry for his clinic, downtown. His absence from the department does not, however, mean that he is unaware of what goes on there and he often summons to his office people (from the most senior professor to the lowest resident), in order to rebuke or congratulate them on things they may have done while he was away, though to this day nobody has found out how the doctor knows what goes on when he isn't there. There is much speculation, of course, but it is truly difficult to be sure that any given person is the source of his information, and the results are amazing, for the physicians in the department work, talk, and laugh as though the doctor were with them. Two of them may, for example, differ—may, indeed, become excited and angry—over the history of how the doctor obtained his doctorate or from which American university he obtained it (even though it is no business of either of them) but they will be certain that whatever they say, like everything else that happens in the department, will be reported to the doctor in detail; and if things are like this when the doctor is not there, just imagine how they are when he is.

Indeed. When the doctor appears, everyone devotes the same energy to doing his work well as he does to staying alive, for the doctor is not given to idle talk. He punishes the wrongdoer whoever he may be and his punishments are immediate and also—like everything he does—extremely strange. Thus if he finds a car parked in his private parking space, he at once orders that its four tires be deflated and then leaves (we may imagine the subsequent difficulties faced by the owner of a car with four flat tires) and if he catches sight of a ward orderly making tea beside the patient's family, he pounces forthwith upon the teakettle and flings it out of the window (it isn't important on whose head the kettle may land; that is the problem of the person passing by in the street). And if the doctor enters the sterilization room and finds that the brush he uses to scrub his hands isn't clean, he will right away hurl it in the face of the nursing sister, and he really does hurl it, meaning that the sister may get her head cut open. (This happened once with a new sister; the others knew from experience how to avoid these flying objects.) And in the operating theater, during those terrifying minutes when the fate of a person lying anaesthetized and with their insides exposed is decided and the doctor's assistants are whispering in dread, the sweat pouring off them in spite of the air conditioning, the doctor—and he alone—remains unflappable, his high-pitched voice rising as he curses the families of those he is working with and insults them with a variety of sentences all of the same structure, as when he says, "Drain the blood, you animal!" or "Call that sewing, you ape?" The surprising thing is that the one insulted—be it surgeon or sister—rather than paying attention to the insult will focus all his thoughts on correcting the mistake. In fact, the doctor doesn't insult his assistants only when angry: he also curses them out when he is pleased and wants to give praise. Thus, at the end of an operation he may say to one of them, "You're a real ass as a surgeon, but you did good work tonight."

Thus, in the doctor's private language the meanings of the insults are changed and the names of animals are employed in the same way that we ordinary mortals might, in our language, use "you."

◈

Hisham worked as he had never worked before. He was on the job every day from seven in the morning to midnight, and on operation days (Sundays and Wednesdays) he would spend the night at the department. When he came home exhausted, he was supposed to find one or two hours in which to review his work for his master. The result was that he didn't get more than four hours sleep a night. His body grew thin, his face pale, and permanent dark rings formed around his eyes. His mother noticed how irritable he was and reproached him frequently for his excessive smoking. At his insistence, she would wake him every day at daybreak, almost weeping out of pity for his weak, exhausted body. Hisham's hard work did not, however, hurt him. What kept him awake was the thought that his hard work might go for nothing. He had a clear well-defined goal in mind—to become one of the great surgeons. Because he was aware that these days would decide his whole future, he was prepared, were there time enough, to double his efforts and, believe it or not, he managed to work with Dr. Bassiouni for a whole year without any disasters. He would go in to see him twice a week to show him the operation schedule and each time Hisham would approach Dr. Bassiouni exactly as we might a live electrical wire, or a gas valve that has to be fixed, meaning that he would extend his hand with the papers and retreat to avoid any impending explosion. Dr. Bassiouni, however, to Hisham's amazement, never exploded. Needless to say, things did not pass without a few special forms of address (Hisham's was usually 'pig') but this was a trifle.

Though Dr. Bassiouni caused Hisham no problems, others brought him a wide variety, and here we should mention that Dr. Bassiouni's department included four other professors, not one of whom enjoyed the same celebrity or authority. Dr. Mansour, for instance had graduated one year after Dr. Bassiouni and like him had a doctorate from America; like him too, he was a skilled surgeon. For reasons that were hard to fathom, however, and as is often the case in life, he did not have the same charisma, and while the presence of Dr. Bassiouni, with his strange appearance, had an effect on people, Dr. Mansour, despite the care he took to wear a three-piece suit summer and winter, resembled, at best, a middle-ranking bureaucrat, meaning that while with his graying hair, his glasses, his good manners, and his soft voice, he was undeniably a respectable person, he was also never anything more than that. Thus there was no great stream of patients to his clinic, since patients usually prefer to contract with a famous surgeon as the latter must obviously be more skilled or how else would he have become famous? And as Dr. Mansour had more free time, it had become his habit to spend most of the day in the department, which he would roam, observing what went on from a distance, and always intervening at the appropriate time. He would, for example, wait until a doctor had prescribed a certain medication for a patient and, as soon as he caught sight of the expression of gratitude in the patient's eyes or heard the patient's family thanking the doctor, would approach and ask the doctor in a low voice what he had prescribed, then give a smile of private (but nevertheless observable) sarcasm and announce to him that what he had prescribed was totally wrong (it never happened that Dr. Mansour found that any doctor had got it right). Nor would Dr. Mansour omit to explain in a clear and audible voice the complications that would follow if the patient were to take that medication, which was known to totally destroy the liver. When, out of the corner of his eye, he noticed the anxiety and confusion on the patient's face, Dr. Mansour would joke with him, saying, "You should praise the Lord! The doctor was going to kill you." At this point the patient and his family would inevitably plead with Dr. Mansour to prescribe another drug for them, so he would take the prescription sheet, resolutely cross out the first medication and then write in another (which usually was no different from the first). Then he would sigh and shake his head, as though to say, "What am I supposed to do about these ignorant doctors, dear God?" and leave exactly as he had come—calmly and politely.

Dr. Mansour would explain these interventions of his by saying "I always pass on my experience to my children" and it was in exactly the same fatherly spirit that Dr. Mansour was accustomed to destroy the hopes of the students whose theses he was supervising. Thus, after the student had worked hard for two whole years on his topic and it was approaching completion, and just as the student was starting to feel stirrings of hope that he might obtain a degree (whether a master's or a doctorate), Dr. Mansour would always discover some fundamental flaw in the study and inform the student of this fact in a deliberate and leisurely fashion (just as you might take your time when sipping mint tea), and then calmly look at the student's face as the frustration and despair took hold and refuse, politely and adamantly, the student's feverish attempts to defend himself. When the student had surrendered to despondency and taken refuge in silence, Dr. Mansour would sigh, with genuine relief, and say, "Don't try to argue about it, my boy. We have at least a year of work ahead of us."

That year would be renewed once, and again, after which Dr. Mansour would frequently advise the student to start over with another supervisor because, quite simply, he was not happy with the study and could not agree to put his name to it. The upshot was that, in twenty years, only four students had persevered to the end and obtained a degree under Dr. Mansour's supervision and the young doctor to whose fate it fell to have Dr. Mansour as an advisor would receive the heartfelt condolences of his colleagues, as though someone dear to him had died. A few days after his appointment, Hisham was invited by Dr. Mansour to attend an operation he was to perform. Hisham was very grateful for this attention, and he scrubbed up and entered with the doctor. The operation was to remove the gall bladder of some wretched peasant from el-Minoufiya and after this had been done, Dr. Mansour asked Hisham to sew up the wound. Hisham focused, controlled the shaking of his hands, and sewed it up as best he knew how. True, his hand was slow, but he made no mistakes, he was certain of that. Afterward, Dr. Mansour asked Hisham to come and see him in his office, invited him to sit, and told him, lighting a cigarette and observing him with the calm of an experienced hunter, "Listen, Hisham. Would you be upset if I told you you'll never do as a surgeon?" Hisham felt fear and asked him what he meant, to which Dr. Mansour replied that being a surgeon was a matter of feeling before it was one of learning and that his long experience allowed him to judge whether the surgical sense was present in a person or not; he had made up his mind to observe him today during the operation and could assert—and for this he was very sorry— that he would never make a surgeon, for which reason he would advise him to go to some other department—internal medicine, for example, or dermatology—where everything depended on training. Hisham burst, as he was expected to, into violent, and then despairing, attempts to convince Dr. Mansour that he was still at the beginning of the road and that he would learn and improve. Dr. Mansour, however, heard Hisham out with head bowed, refused his arguments with one short sentence, then drove him with another to a further attempt to convince him, and so on, until Dr. Mansour had had his fill of Hisham's chagrin and despair and stood up, bringing the meeting to a close by saying, in a soft well-mannered voice, "I hope to hear of your resignation in the near future. I'm sorry, but I'm acting for your own good."

❖

"A few minutes aren't enough to judge me, and nobody has the authority to force me to resign," Hisham told himself. This convinced him and he calmed down and decided to put what Dr. Mansour had said out of his mind and treat it as though it had never happened. Despite this, for weeks he would get confused whenever he was entrusted with a task during an operation; Dr. Mansour's words would spring insistently into his mind, his hands would shake, and he would have to expend extraordinary effort not to botch things. In any case, Hisham stopped helping Dr. Mansour in his operations after that. Indeed, he started taking steps so that he wouldn't even see him and if he caught sight of him coming down the hall, would go into a side room and busy himself with something until he had passed. Once it seemed to him that Dr. Mansour saw him, and was smiling. Hisham took to helping the other professors thereafter and was amazed to find that each of them, in his own way, treated him badly. At first, he thought that they must hate him for some reason but he soon discovered that he was not being targeted personally but that relations among everybody were bad: the head sister was always telling the other sisters off and the professors accused everybody—nursing sisters and doctors—of ignorance and poor performance. In a word, everyone had taken it upon himself to expose the ignorance of those who were junior to him, and the quarrels proceeded as in some monotonous soap opera. In the morning, a professor would be rude to a lecturer and tell him off in front of everybody and half an hour later the lecturer would find a fatal mistake made by an assistant lecturer, who would lose no time in his turn in taking it out on a resident or a sister. As Hisham was the most junior, the flood of affronts would always end up pouring down on his head. Fearing a confrontation that Dr. Bassiouni might hear about, Hisham would accept the slights in silence, or, if his tormentor went too far, would direct at him a sad and reproachful smile. He thought at first that this approach would get him out of all the things that he had to put up with, but the actual result was that the insults multiplied and everyone in the department started shouting at Hisham and finding fault with him for the most insignificant reasons. Hisham even caught the sisters, who were beneath him in the hierarchy, winking more than once to one another over him and laughing. This pained him, and each night before he slept, Hisham would put the pillow over his head and remember, with bitter feelings, the events of the day. He would counsel himself to be patient, saying, "It will all change. I will become more skillful. I will make first place in the master's exam and then they will think hard before doing that. In fact, nobody will dare to speak to me without using my title."

The fact is that this poisonous, hatred-charged atmosphere did not prevent Hisham from learning. He read up well on each case and focused his mind during the operations, staring at everything he saw so as to fix it in his memory; thus he inevitably made progress. His diagnostic mistakes gradually grew fewer and he became certain that, were he allowed, he could perform numerous operations with success. As the master's exam approached, Hisham realized that this was his big chance. He closeted himself with his books, reading, understanding, and memorizing. Often morning would find him still studying, on which occasions he would take a cold shower to wake himself up and then go to the department without having slept. Hisham passed the written exam with virtually no mistakes, did perfectly on the practical, and, as was his custom, won the admiration of the examiners on the oral. When Hisham finished, he was certain of the result.

An unintentional mistake resulted in the omission of his name from the list of those who had passed, or so Hisham decided. He did not therefore worry too much and went to the Office of Student Affairs, where he explained things to the director. The man was extremely polite and Hisham got to see his grades in the exam. Hisham didn't argue or say anything, but set off immediately for Dr. Bassiouni's office. He knocked quickly and hard on the door, opened it, and went in. Dr. Bassiouni was reading. Hisham interrupted him, saying in a hoarse, panting voice (which surprised Hisham himself), "I failed the exam."

"Congratulations," said Dr. Bassiouni without lifting his eyes from what he was reading.

"I want to know why I failed," Hisham insisted obstinately.

"You failed because you didn't deserve to succeed," Dr.

Bassiouni told Hisham, starting to fiddle with his long side-burns. His tone gave warning of a coming eruption.

"I had no mistakes on my written or my practical. And the oral . . . ."

At this, Dr. Bassiouni exploded. "Listen, pig. Do you think I'm taking time out from my many tasks so that I can repeat to you what I tell you every day? I've told you a thousand times: there is a difference between the surgery exam and the primary school certificate. We don't let everyone who turns up become a surgeon, no matter how much he knows. What matters to us is your character and above all your morals. I've told you from the beginning, you will never succeed and continue with us unless you please me. Got it?"

Hisham took refuge in silence.

"Now, be about your business, pig."

And Hisham left. He resumed his work as usual and when he was alone that night he wasn't exactly sad; it was a feeling of panic that possessed him. Panic is the right word because, for the first time, he realized that his intelligence, that firm base on which he had always confidently depended, was no longer valid. That the doctor had clearly announced that he did not please him (wasn't that what he'd said?) when he did not know what to do in order to make him pleased further increased his agitation. Days passed, and weeks, and months, and Hisham went on working in the department with his old application but with only half his mind, the other half being preoccupied with the urgent and critical question, what could he do to please Dr. Bassiouni? When Hisham could come up with no answer, he decided to ask the people he knew, starting with his mother, so he put the question to her. His mother, however—to his amazement—attributed all his problems to his colleagues' envy of his superiority and took to pestering him every evening to pass seven times over a brazier for which she brought incense from the tomb of Lady Sugar Lump (a well-known saint with a shrine on el-Azhar Street). Hisham's annoyance at all this was extreme, but he did it to please his mother and shut her up, submitting and passing seven times over the brazier. Time went by, and there were only months to go before the second master's exam (and Hisham's last chance). He was desperate to know how to please Dr. Bassiouni and started getting to know every professor in the department, working out the times when he was in his best mood, and then getting him on his own and telling him fawningly, "I would like to benefit from your experience, Professor. What should I do to make Dr. Bassiouni pleased?" To which, as one, they would smilingly reply, "Our professor, Dr. Bassiouni, loves anyone who gives himself wholly and sincerely to his work." Hisham knew that they were lying and started asking his colleagues in the other departments. He would enter the radiology department or walk to the pathology department, look around for an old fellow student, and put the question to him. Gradually, Hisham started presenting his problem to doctors he didn't know: he would go up to them smiling, introduce himself, and then go over the matter, posing the question, "What should I do to please Dr. Bassiouni?"

No one knows exactly how Hisham happened across the answer because what happened then happened so suddenly. On Sunday, Hisham went in as usual to go over the list of operations with Dr. Bassiouni, a process that normally took

only a few minutes. This time, however, Hisham stayed . . .
and stayed . . . until, after an hour had passed since he'd
gone in, the doctors in the department started whispering to
one another in anxiety and surprise. Eventually, Hisham came
out, his face wearing a strange expression that was a mixture
of pain, exhaustion, and relief. No one knows what passed
between Hisham and Dr. Bassiouni on that day, but equally
no one ever forgot that meeting of theirs because it was the
beginning of the transformation. After this, Hisham would
go in to Dr. Bassiouni every day and spend a long time with
him. Indeed, Dr. Bassiouni would send someone to look for
him if he did not come, and within a few weeks it was widely
reported in the department that the doctor had taken Hisham
to help him in his private clinic (which was something Dr.
Bassiouni hadn't done with a resident for years). Thenceforth
Hisham became the sole person charged with taking care of
Dr. Bassiouni's appointments and availability and if you
wanted to know in what hospital Dr. Bassiouni would be
performing an operation tomorrow or whether he was in the
mood to allow you to present your request to him, you
would have to ask Hisham, and only Hisham. Nor did
Hisham any longer have to put up with anyone's abuse, for
the simple reason that no one abused him any longer. On the
contrary, everyone, great and small, started treating him
nicely; even Dr. Mansour took to making a point of finding
him every morning to say hello and he asked him more than
once to assist him with his operations, though Hisham
would decline, excusing himself on the grounds that his time
was completely taken up with "the Pasha" (that is, Bassiouni),
on hearing which Dr. Mansour would nod his head as

though he completely understood just how busy Hisham must be. It wasn't long before Hisham gained a reputation as a strict resident who would countenance no slacking where work was concerned and dock days from any sister who made a mistake, after first giving her a dressing down. If the mistake was made by a senior doctor in the department, Hisham would look at him, smile (politely and broadly), and ask him, "Do you think the Pasha would be happy to hear that you are doing that?" (a question that would agitate even the most confident and severe among them). And when Hisham took the master's exam for the second time, he didn't bother to closet himself with his books like the time before, but passed and took first place, and Dr. Bassiouni, before the results were made public, congratulated him with the words, "Well done, pig. You've come out at the top." Hisham smiled and bowed, his smile and his movements seeming this time to be of a new and different kind, and said, "I owe it all to you, Pasha."

His colleagues and professors made a big fuss over congratulating Hisham but when the time came for him to be appointed, the university administration announced that there were no empty posts. Such a problem could have been enough to destroy Hisham's future but, as soon as he heard the news, early in the morning, he picked up the phone and called Dr. Bassiouni at home (which is something no one had ever dared to do before) and Dr. Bassiouni quite understood the situation and immediately contacted the relevant people, and before midday, Hisham had received the news of his appointment as an assistant lecturer in the department of general surgery.

All this happened two or more years ago. Now Hisham is busy preparing his doctoral thesis (under Dr. Bassiouni's supervision) and we—his former fellow students—are forever delighting in his achievement. Frequently we visit him at the surgery department, where we have a lovely time with him, chatting and recalling old memories, though sometimes, despite the cheerful welcome he gives us, and despite our affection for and pride in him, we feel that something about our old friend has changed. It is, however, a thought that we quickly expel from our minds.

And We Have Covered Their Eyes

WHO DOESN'T KNOW MR. GOUDA? Doubtless, most of us do. If someone hasn't found themself a colleague of Mr. Gouda's at work or during their studies, they will surely have come across him on a crowded bus or, and this is even more likely, will have seen him with a bag of groceries under his arm breaking up some fight that has broken out in the line at the government food co-op, or perhaps listened to the lecture on soccer that Mr. Gouda is accustomed to deliver every Friday evening at the café.

At the very least, all of us will have observed Mr. Gouda on his daily morning journey with his three children, each of whom he delivers to their respective school before hurrying to the Ministry of Planning, where he is employed in the Monitoring Department.

In any case, I'm writing only for those who know Mr. Gouda. Those who haven't met him will never understand what he represents.

❖

Never did he feel embarrassed about his shoes. They were made of cloth, but he always claimed that this kind of shoe was easy on his feet. In fact, Mr. Gouda would sometimes express to anyone who might care to listen his amazement at how other people could stand wearing leather shoes in such terrible heat.

Likewise, thanks to the efforts of his wife, Busayna, his pants always looked fairly smart.

The problem was the shirts. Mr. Gouda owned three, which he wore in rotation through the week, and the white one was threadbare. If it had been torn, Mr. Gouda could have dispensed with it altogether, but it was merely threadbare, meaning that it had that certain scratchiness that afflicts a shirt once it has become worn out and the little threads that emerge and dangle free of the weave. Despite this, on some gray and gloomy days, Mr. Gouda was compelled to wear the white shirt, and last Thursday was one of those days.

That morning, Mr. Gouda's behavior changed completely.

It may seem an exaggerated reaction, but I have to tell those who have not experienced the effect of a threadbare shirt on a man's behavior that when Mr. Gouda spoke to his colleagues that morning, it was in almost inaudible tones and when he ordered his morning coffee, he was more than usually polite, saying, "A medium-sweet coffee, if you'd be so kind, Borai," instead of uttering his normal shout of, "Medium-sweet, Borai!"

I also have to tell you that Mr. Gouda spent most of the day behind his desk pretending to occupy himself with files of no importance. He responded tersely to the chatter of his colleagues and found himself more than normally predisposed to agree with the opinions of those who spoke to him; even soccer, Mr. Gouda's favorite topic of conversation, failed to engage his interest that morning. Mr. Gouda felt mortified and was so embarrassed he couldn't decide where to put his hands, sometimes placing them on the desk, sometimes letting them hang at his sides, and finally folding them over his chest, in which position he tried his best to keep them for the rest of the day. No one knows why Mr. Gouda yielded to an irresistible desire to examine his colleagues' clothes so closely but whenever he noticed that one of them was looking shabby, Mr. Gouda would feel a secret, guilty relief.

It was indeed a wearisome day, and it would have been—I repeat, would have been—possible for the day to have passed without anything further happening to increase Mr. Gouda's anxiety and distress, but it seems that it is by evil laws that the world is governed, for at about one o'clock a handsome, smartly dressed young man of not more than thirty entered the Monitoring Department and directed his steps straight toward the desk of Mr. Gouda. He was carrying papers that he wanted to have stamped—and stamping papers was about all that Mr. Gouda's job consisted of—and Mr. Gouda got the stamp out of the drawer, as he always did, and prepared himself to stamp. Mr. Gouda has often, subsequently, thought about what the young man did, and has come up with the following interpretation: the youth belonged to a certain category of men who carry about with them something vaguely feminine, something unshakeable that one does not notice at first but which reveals itself as soon as one asks one of them, for example, about the price of cloth, or he boasts of his skill as a cook or at buying fruit, or takes longer than necessary to polish his glasses. Anyway, Mr. Gouda quickly finished stamping the papers but the young man was polite and friendly—as most men of that sort are— and a delightful conversation sprang up between the young man and Mr. Gouda that lasted some minutes. When the young man got up to go, Mr. Gouda pressed him strongly to stay and the young man sat down again, his face wearing a warm and open expression, and gave Mr. Gouda a cigarette of an imported brand, which Mr. Gouda kissed in grateful acceptance, and the pleasure of smoking the cigarette added still further to the agreeable atmosphere. A warm sensation stole into Mr. Gouda's heart and he forgot all about his shirt and removed his hands from his chest and found a place to put them on either side of his chair. Eventually, being eager to show his friendliness, Mr. Gouda stood up and made a show of looking for the office boy so that he could order some refreshment for "the gentleman." All of a sudden one of the young man's feminine avatars possessed him and, crying out, "Just a moment, my dear Mr. Gouda!" he stood up and gazed intently at Mr. Gouda's shirt, and then, without saying a word, stretched out his hand and with slender, well-schooled fingers plucked a thread off the white shirt. Then he looked at Mr. Gouda and gave him an innocent smile.

The young man hadn't meant anything by the gesture. It was his custom to reach out to other people's clothes and fasten an undone button or pluck off an unwanted thread. He liked everything to look proper. He couldn't bear to do nothing about a twisted collar or allow a badly tied necktie to pass.

Sometimes, when he caught sight of a small leaf sticking to the hair of the man he was talking to, he would even, whoever it might be, reach out an arm, pull his head toward him, and set to searching through his hair with his fingers until he could pick out the offending leaf and fling it away. Then, and only then, he would sigh contentedly and ask his interlocutor with the greatest politeness, "What were you saying, my dear sir?"

That was the way the young man was. He couldn't imagine that the removal of a silly thread could possibly upset anyone. And in fact Mr. Gouda didn't display any appreciable annoyance in front of the young man. Later, however, when waiting ages for the bus, when he raised his daily paper to shield his bald head from the sun, when he managed (with a skill born of practice) to leap onto and stuff his fat body inside the crammed vehicle, he felt an oppressive sensation bearing down on his chest and, one by one, Mr. Gouda's cares welled up, overflowed, and violently burst their banks. He was forty-five years old. An employee in the Monitoring Department at the Ministry of Planning. His main job was to stamp papers—numerous papers which, the years had taught him, possessed neither use nor significance.

Often, Mr. Gouda would catch sight of companions from his school days riding in luxury cars or read about their doings in the press, and when he encountered these glittering successes he'd always hope in his heart that one of them would treat him with arrogance and scorn, that one of them would mock him or scoff at his poverty and failure, that one of them, in a word, would give him a reasonable excuse to vent his spleen against him, but it never happened. They treated him with excessive kindness and politeness.

117

They put him at his ease when talking to him, laughed long at his witticisms, and listened to him with interest, exactly like the good-hearted sultan who halts his mighty procession and, seized by pity, hurries over to a weeping child or poor widow. This would cause Mr. Gouda's anxieties to overwhelm him completely.

Now, I have to stress that the story of the cigarette kiosk was an odd one and that Mr. Gouda was used to telling it in the café to make his friends laugh. They all loved the story and often asked him to repeat it, at which moment he would feel true ecstasy and, taking a deep drag on his cigarette, would tell it over again, each repetition adding to his skillfulness in the telling, as he focused like a master on the funniest parts, so that his friends' enjoyment became intense, their laughter raucous. And Mr. Gouda always laughed along with them.

This time, however, Mr. Gouda recalled the story of the cigarette kiosk and found nothing in it to laugh about. On the contrary, embarrassment and distress swept over him as he thought back over the day when his wife had convinced him that most millionaires had started by selling cigarettes and candy. He remembered how he had struggled, and gone on struggling, until he'd acquired a cigarette kiosk in a Cairo suburb, how he'd used to leave work and go and stand in the kiosk surrounded by the cartons of cigarettes and packets of cookies, and how the kiosk, which was built of metal, would grow hotter and hotter in the heat of the sun until it was burning like a furnace, with Mr. Gouda inside it, waiting for customers and wealth.

And finally Mr. Gouda remembered how he'd discovered, after three whole months, that they'd tricked him and that the area had no customers. By the time his memories had carried him along to that point, he'd reached the house.

No one at home noticed any sign of dejection on his face. He took off his street clothes as soon as he entered the house and joked around with the kids, as usual, picking up Sherif, the youngest, by his little feet and raising him until his hands touched the ceiling, and he went on doing this until the little fellow broke out into rapid and continuous fits of laughter. Then he went into the kitchen, asked for the food to be brought in a hurry and joked a lot with his wife, even pinching her more than once. He was entirely normal.

Mr. Gouda did only one thing that was strange. It occurred after lunch, when he and Busayna sought their bed for a little rest. It was stiflingly hot, and Mr. Gouda and his wife were dripping with sweat, despite which, and despite the fact that it was not his habit to have relations with her in the middle of the day, he asked for her and, very naturally, she refused, saying, "I'm tired, Gouda, and it's hot." Mr. Gouda, however, kept insisting until in the end she gave in and he flung himself onto her in a hot, violent encounter, wallowing and losing himself and producing a strong and copious performance. Busayna knew him. He was never like that unless he was very happy or very sad.

When Mr. Gouda had finished, he collapsed on his side, exhausted, and soon he covered his head with the pillow. He didn't go to sleep, though, and some minutes of silence passed. By the time that he let out a heart-felt sigh, Busayna had decided to intervene.

"What's worrying you, Gouda?"

There were so many things he would have liked to talk about that he said nothing.

"You don't want to tell me? Come on, you don't really think I'm going to go to sleep and leave you all upset like this, do you?"

"It's the way I look, Busayna. I don't look right at all any more, Busayna."

At first, she didn't hear, and when he repeated the same sentence, she didn't understand a thing.

"To be honest, I don't understand," she said.

"I'm telling you, it's my clothes. My clothes have got really awful. Especially the shirts. The shirt I was wearing today was a disaster."

He expected her to answer him with any old thing that might come to her mind, but he never expected her to laugh. But Busayna did laugh. She went on laughing until the bed rocked beneath her. Mr. Gouda's surprise turned to extreme annoyance and he shouted, "What are you laughing at? I'm telling you I don't have any clothes to wear."

"I'm laughing so that you'll know just what a treasure your Bussy is."

Mr. Gouda didn't understand. Her voice continued, with new strength: "You're a lucky devil to have married a woman like me."

"Meaning what?"

"My dear good Mr. Gouda, I've known for ages that you don't have any shirts, and so I joined a savings co-op. And Thursday next, God willing, we're going to take a trip to Port Said and buy everything you need.* Now do you understand?"

---

* Port Said is located in the Suez Canal duty-free zone.

From that Thursday to the next the days were all color and excitement, but Mr. Gouda was a sensible man. He dreamed, it's true, of the coming Thursday and a tender, naughty smile would, it's true, leap, despite his best efforts, to his lips whenever he pictured himself roaming the department's corridors in his smart new shirt. At the same time, however, he understood very well that he'd have to go on paying into the co-op for a whole year, during which he would have to deduct a part of his salary to pay the price of that day. Mr. Gouda therefore thought everything over carefully and left nothing to chance. What would he buy from Port Said? Where exactly would he go? How would he deal with the officer at Customs? Which pocket, indeed, would he put his money in while he was on the outward journey? Dozens of minute details engaged Mr. Gouda's attention and were studied exhaustively by him, until in the end he had everything ready in his mind and the time to act had arrived.

On the morning of the Wednesday before, Mr. Gouda announced to his colleagues at the Monitoring Department that he wouldn't be coming in the following day. When they asked him why not, he started leafing through the file that was in front of him on his desk and then said, out of the corner of his mouth and as though it had nothing to do with him, "Oh, it's nothing really. I was just thinking of going to Port Said tomorrow, you know."

Within less than half an hour, the news of Mr. Gouda's trip to Port Said had spread among the employees and he was inundated with requests of every description—shirts, socks, beauty products. Mr. Gouda knew full well that he wouldn't buy any of them but he refused no one nevertheless.

He would listen and then say, with that air of importance of which he had felt so long deprived, "God willing. I'll do my very best to remember."

How happy he was too when he entered the office of Mr. Allouba, the department's director, and asked him if there was anything he'd like from Port Said.

Mr. Gouda's pleasure increased further when his boss responded, in a pleasant and gentle voice, "Before all else, your safe return, of course, Gouda. Though, actually, there is a kind of chocolate that my wife is very fond of. You know how women are, Gouda." Allouba chuckled, and followed with a loud clearing of his throat to restore his dignity.

That Wednesday, Mr. Gouda was an important personage, but when, at night, he betook himself to bed, he was seized by an obscure feeling, a foolish feeling both illogical and baseless, that inspired in him the notion that he would never get to Port Said. Everything was ready. He had the money and had even familiarized himself with the prices. The next day he would go—what could prevent him? All the same, that darkly seductive voice kept on whispering at him and it was only with the greatest difficulty that Mr. Gouda managed to rid himself of his imaginings and go to sleep.

In the morning, when he woke up, he felt somewhat terrified as he counted his money for the last time, then folded the bundle of notes carefully and put it into his pants pocket, making sure that it had gone all the way down to the bottom. When Mr. Gouda and his wife took their seats on the bus headed for Port Said, Busayna recited the opening chapter of the Qur'an in a low voice, and the moment they arrived in Port Said, Mr. Gouda put his plan into action.

He had written down the things he needed on a small piece of paper. The names of the stores were written on another, separate, piece of paper, which saved Mr. Gouda and his wife a great deal of wandering, so that by the middle of the day they were done with their shopping.

There were some household items for Busayna, while Mr. Gouda had acquired four new shirts, one of them with red and white vertical stripes. This shirt was particularly elegant.

The couple having found a discreet refuge in the lobby of one of the city's smart apartment buildings, Mr. Gouda took off, for the last time, his old white shirt and exchanged it for one of the new ones, while Busayna succeeded in hiding two more shirts inside the folds of her clothes. This meant that just one shirt was left, which Mr. Gouda carried in his hand. The two were then ready to enter Customs, where they had to stand at the end of a long line of people without cars waiting for the inspector.

When their turn approached, when they were within a few paces of the inspector, Busayna bent toward her husband and whispered in his ear, and Mr. Gouda's voice, filled with anguish and anxiety, was soon to be heard, uttering the words, "In the Name of God, the Merciful, the Compassionate," and then proceeding to recite, in genuine holy dread, new shirt in hand, *"And We have put before them a barrier and behind them a barrier; and We have covered their eyes so they do not see . . . and We have covered their eyes so they do not see . . . and We have covered their eyes so they do not see. . . ."**

---

* *This scripture is from the Qur'an 36:9.*

123

To the Air Conditioning Attendant of the Hall

DEAR MR. AIR CONDITIONING ATTENDANT, pray listen closely as I start my tale.

My tale, my dear Attendant, is a boorish Arab tale that knows not how to behave. The ladies and gentlemen present in the hall will be afflicted by rage when I speak. Fury will ignite in their hearts, and for this reason I must beg you, my dear Air Conditioning Attendant, to turn up the cooling from time to time.

And you, my dear Sound Engineer, when I start to speak, seek to divert the attention of the listeners from me. Give them, my dear Engineer, yet more loud music.

As for you, my dear Acrobat, you must entertain the ones that grow furious. Fall flat on your face or walk on your hands. If necessary, Acrobat, let forth a cry like the braying of a donkey. What matters is that good cheer be unconfined, and anger dispelled.

❖

Ladies and gentlemen,

My story starts with a bit of bad luck, the sort of wretched ill-fortune that brings an innocent child into this world with a disfigured face or body, the sort of unjust fate that bereaves the tender-hearted father of his youthful son and sows cancer in the breast of the up-and-coming man.

Such a black fate it was that made Jenin an Arab city. Had Jenin been located in Switzerland, had its orange groves been covered with the sparkling snows of Europe, had its many mosques been Catholic churches, had the people of Jenin belonged to the superior, white-skinned race, or had Jenin not known—God forbid—the chanting of the Qur'an or the performance of the five daily prayers, what befell it would never have done so. Blind fate, however, created Jenin an Arab city and, not content with this ignominy, made it a Palestinian city to boot. Finally, that no humiliation might be spared, fate chose to set it on the West Bank, right on the border with the respected Jewish State. Yet let God, High and Omnipotent, bear witness—as do the reports of the various intelligence agencies—that not one of the people of Jenin was given to wanton acts of violence. It was both small city and large house, and its people were peaceable.

The good-natured peasants were skilled at the growing of oranges, and that was all they knew. They were careful to say their Friday prayers and they loved to drink arak.

Nor did it ever happen that anyone from Jenin was heard to raise his voice or say a foul word, not even in the days of folly, when black thoughts about Israel ran like poison in the veins of the Arab world and when the Arabs where addicted to talk of the liberation of Palestine, socialism, nationalism, and other such bunkum. Even in those days, Jenin remained the same, and the people of Jenin set off, as they always had done, to the orange groves, knowing nothing else, to cultivate and harvest.

Truth to tell, this good conduct had a considerable impact on the hearts of the Jewish authorities—so much so in fact that they considered a number of times presenting a large reward to their peaceable neighbors, and indeed this almost came to pass, and would have done so, had there not occurred the unfortunate, the most extremely unfortunate, events that Jenin witnessed during the spring of 1967.

Dear Mr. Air Conditioning Attendant, one degree colder, if you please.

I shall relate what happened all at one go.

In May 1967, Jenin decided to enter the war. Picture, good people, the farmers of Jenin bearing weapons and setting off to fight. And to fight whom? The State of Israel. Surely, it is an ironic fate that drives man to seek his demise with his own hand.

Flat on your face, Acrobat!

June 1967 began, and the crisis deepened and dug in its heels and war was on everybody's lips. On a day as terrible as the sun and as towering as a mountain, the Jordanian army took a deep breath, raised its mighty arm, and entered Jenin.* This was according to plan, because Jenin was on the front line and the Jordanians had to move into it in order to defend it.

From 1948 to 1967, the Palestinian territories east of the armistice line with Israel and west of the River Jordan (the 'West Bank') were under Jordanian rule.

Jenin will never forget that day. "Welcome, Heroes of Jordan!" read the broad banners that dangled proudly as they waited and the men assembled in the narrow lanes. Some sat. Others were unable to do so, so great was the yearning, and they went up to the hilltop, returning with exciting news: "In half an hour the heroes will be here! They may already be on the outskirts!" Meanwhile the women had made themselves busy that day as on no other—and how could it not be so, when the heroes would arrive after a hard journey and must find something ready to eat and drink? And that something was produced. Dozens of sandwiches, fried pastries, casseroles, and every other kind of dish were born, along with bottles of arak in long rows, nestled in palm-leaf wrappers.

Even the children in Jenin were looking forward to the arrival of the Jordanian army with the greatest zeal, the children having their own reasons, which included seeing a real army in the flesh, and rifles, for the first time—an army next to which those of Metro-Goldwyn-Mayer would look like a bunch of outmoded and badly made toys.

What a lovely dance, dear Sound Engineer!

The Jordanian army arrived at one o'clock in the afternoon and the appearance of the first soldier at the edge of the city and the sight of his green uniform and shining brass badge were the signal, the magic signal, for the release of all the emotions that had been waiting since the morning—all in one outburst and at one time. The ululations of joy, the plaudits, the patriotic songs, and the shouts broke out. Veritable showers of welcoming roses were thrown over heads. The heroes had come to defend Jenin and all Jenin embraced the heroes. Everyone sang and waved and no one felt embarrassed to express their feelings—it was a moment of truth that permitted no standing on ceremony. Even the sheikhs and notables were hurrahing. Every individual in Jenin was careful to make sure that their greeting—their own personal greeting—reached the warriors, and all these greetings seemingly came together into one great greeting. And, truth be told, the Jordanian army, with its awe-inspiring military formations and angry black weapons, merited such enthusiasm. Its men were men, with huge, muscle-bound bodies and Arab mustaches "sturdy enough for a hawk to sit on" (without misgivings). The whole scene spoke of power, and when the first tank appeared it all became too much to bear, and everyone rushed forward to climb the steel walls, and the topknot of a tank opened and a warrior poked his head up, laughing and accepting hugs and kisses.

In a few minutes the entire column had broken ranks and the soldiers were swept up with the natives in an irresistible popular demonstration. Shoulders competed in sincere desire to be the ones to carry the heroes of Jordan and the crowds overflowed the lanes of Jenin, ending up in the square of the Great Mosque (Jenin's largest), where the preacher, finding himself in a unprecedented situation, in no way fell short of the required ardor, organizing everyone into rows and leading a one-of-a-kind prayer, as to whose religious propriety no one gave a hoot, and then delivered a fiery sermon, whole chunks of which he would repeat in subsequent years to his children. To start, the preacher spoke of the first of the Prophet's followers who migrated to Medina and of those who supported his cause there.

Then he shifted to the concept of holy struggle in Islam. By the time he came to the verse of the Qur'an that says, "*O believers, if you help God, He will help you*," things had slipped out of his control and the prayerful masses were transformed into a veritable volcano of cheering and shouts of "God is Great!"

It was a day of truth in the life of Jenin. In the evening, the enthusiasm did not flag but became somewhat calmer and the commander of the Jordanian forces, whom they called the Officer in Command (such was his rank), met with the sheikhs and leading men of Jenin to go over arrangements for the defense of the city. Those gathered there spoke of certain ancient canons situated on the high hill and the meeting broke up quickly, the sheikhs and notables emerging well-satisfied to reassure the people and bring them the glad tidings of the clear impending victory.

Thus it was, good people, that Jenin lived June 4, 1967, and on that night, the night of June 4 and 5, 1967, the people of Jenin slept, as they had to, calmly, their breathing regular. When war broke out the following day, the people received the news of the fighting with high spirits and unshakeable optimism. How could anyone be afraid? How could anyone think, even for an instant, of anything less than total victory, or of retreat? How could such a thing be, when the day was to be one of victory? The day was a day of victory—God's hand guided ours, we would crush them—and on that day too we would destroy the Jewish State and its citizens would be scattered once more to the ends of the earth. This was a reality of scriptural certainty; if it were not, then what was the meaning of Abdel Nasser? What was the meaning of the heroes of Jordan, thirsting to rip apart the Jews? How, otherwise, were we to interpret the communiqués from Cairo about Israeli planes dropping like flies? Could all this mean any but one thing? And for a whole hour, on the morning of June 5, from nine o'clock to ten o'clock, a rosy hour granted by God in His mercy, all hearts enjoyed their victory over Israel. And what a victory! A final and absolute victory, a mighty victory from days of old that brought with it memories of Hattin and the sword of Khalid combined with the battle cries of the first Muslim conquests.* But such moments of happiness pass quickly, like dreams, and in Jenin, as the clock struck ten, the time of dismay arrived.

Turn the cooling dial all the way up, my dear sir. The sweat is starting to drip.

It all started with a foolish word, a silly rumor that no one could repeat without sarcasm but which, to the amazement of all, kept going, spreading and becoming more insistent until the whispering in the lanes of Jenin was transformed into clear and pitiful cries: "The Jordanians are withdrawing." Until the last moment the people remained half in belief, half in denial and doubt, until the Officer in Command appeared, gathered a goodly number of the sheikhs, and informed them of the new orders: "The Jordanian army will withdraw from Jenin." When the people asked him why, he answered curtly, "The plan of defense has changed."

"And who will protect Jenin, sir?"

---

* *Hattin was the site of Saladin's victory over the Crusaders in 1187 that restored Jerusalem to Muslim rule. Khalid ibn al-Walid (592–642), also known as 'the Sword of God,' commander of the Muslim forces during their early conquests, remained undefeated in over a hundred battles.*

At this, the Officer in Command almost lost his temper. "I can assure you that we are not simpletons," he said. "We know exactly what we are doing. We shall withdraw, and then an entire division of the Iraqi army will come and defend the city."

For the second, and last, time, the Jordanians drew themselves up in their implacable ranks and shouldered their choleric weapons. Then they began their withdrawal.

We report both the positive and the negative. Thanks to the skills and long experience of the Officer in Command, the withdrawal from Jenin took place with notable alacrity, and the people of Jenin stood and watched, surrendering one and all to a deep silence that was simultaneously both restful and eloquent. The chains of the withdrawing tanks grated over the earth, creating a doleful rattling sound, and from time to time (one knows not whether to laugh or cry) a passing breeze would gust over the withdrawing forces causing one of the broad banners proclaiming "Welcome, Heroes of Jordan" to move over their heads.

❖

Ladies and gentlemen,

I must reaffirm that my story is innocent of any ill intent or slander. If the people of Jenin did not understand—and still do not understand—why the Jordanian army withdrew and left them on the morning of June 5, that is perfectly natural, for soldiers have their rules and their regulations, which must of necessity lie beyond the ken of the minds of naive growers of oranges. Whatever happened or didn't happen, God forbid that the Officer in Command should have lied or erred; by the

131

same token, let God bear witness that everything the Officer in Command prophesied would happen did happen, and exactly as he prophesied it. Not an hour had passed after the Jordanian withdrawal before Iraqi tanks arrived, come to defend Jenin in accordance with the plan. But it seems there must have been some kind of mix-up, for the moment the Iraqi tanks got close to Jenin, they started shelling.

A minor mishap of the sort that happens all the time in war! The Iraqi tanks went on shelling Jenin until they had razed it to the ground. Then the negligible mistake was made complete, and Jewish soldiers descended from the Iraqi tanks and entered Jenin, which, to this day, they haven't left.

On the evening of June 6, 1967, when Major Levy was appointed military governor of the city of Jenin, one of the sheikhs, wanting to have a joke with him, told him the story of the Iraqi tanks, and when Major Levy discovered that the people of Jenin had been on the verge of welcoming the tanks with roses, he removed his pipe from his mouth, jerked his body backward, and then burst out laughing so hard that he ended up coughing and weeping.

❖

My dear Air Conditioning Attendant of the hall,
My dear Sound Engineer,
My dear Acrobat,
My thanks to you all.
Now my boorish Arab tale is done, and the ladies and gentlemen seated in the hall are still enjoying the air conditioning.

An Administrative Order

HIS NAME, IN FULL, WAS 'UNCLE IBRAHIM' and despite his poverty and pallid face, a surprisingly large paunch hung through the opening of his threadbare coat. While a paunch is considered among the middle classes a medical condition to be treated by diet and exercise, and merchants regard it as a palpable indication of blessings whose constant presence is to be desired, the paunches of the poor are and ever will be mere swellings that they carry around for no obvious reason.

Uncle Ibrahim's shameless paunch had ruined him a full set of clothes that the doctors at the hospital had bought him the year before.

The records give Worker Muhammad Ibrahim's job as 'cleaner,' at a wage of twenty pounds and thirty piasters precisely per month, but because Uncle Ibrahim was a kindly man with a cheerful manner, and because he was clean (and cleanliness was very important), the doctors had chosen him to make the coffee and tea, replacing Uncle Salih, who had retired.

Life thus became intermittently bearable. Given that Uncle Ibrahim had no other duties than his new job of "doing the tea and coffee" he would earn in tips more than half again over and above his basic wages. This enabled him to smoke as he wished, buy gallabiyas and shoes for his children (of whom the eldest was ten), and purchase a small piece of hashish so that he could prolong the act of sex with his wife. Uncle Ibrahim was even able (this happened twice) to pay for a place in a shared taxi when he was late for work.

Uncle Ibrahim counted on his thick fingers "five years of living decently"—living decently meaning that a soul didn't have to beg; five years of "blessings for which we thank God." And whatever he might do on a Thursday night, which was his wife's preferred time for staying up late, Uncle Ibrahim was careful to be in the little mosque for the Friday prayer, and was accustomed to go there with clean body and clothes, and smelling good.

When the sermon started, Uncle Ibrahim would take his head in his hands and lower his eyes. One day, after a heated sermon on alms-giving, Uncle Ibrahim became aware of a guilty unease and made up his mind to do something, and thereafter he made a habit of selecting one of the hospital's penniless patients and making coffee for him for nothing.

Uncle Ibrahim was a good man.

❖

As the preacher at the mosque often said, nothing lasts forever.

134

A few months later, Worker Muhammad Ibrahim received an administrative order assigning him to the hospital gate, the supervisor saying as he handed it to him, "Congratulations, Ibrahim. Now you're on the security staff." Ibrahim felt an obscure sense of panic, but the scene played itself out and he took receipt of a black wool overcoat and huge military boots and started standing every day at the hospital gate, keeping out the visitors and saluting the doctors as they entered in their cars. For the first month, the smell of tea and hot water tormented Uncle Ibrahim, and he also had no choice but to beg, so he started talking all the time about his children's illnesses and how they were falling behind at school. The doctors' smiles turned tepid. "God willing, He will find you a way, Uncle Ibrahim," they would say.

The second month, Uncle Ibrahim went to his supervisor and put a stop to his begging with the words, "I want to go back," and the supervisor quietly raised his hand and removed his glasses, as he pronounced in a hateful voice, "It's an administrative order, Ibrahim."

The third month, Uncle Ibrahim changed greatly. He stopped greeting the doctors as they entered in their cars. He took to sitting on his seat by the gate and holding his black coat tightly closed. His face acquired a fixed expression and his looks turned hard and unrelenting.

Those who were present at the scene say that the old lady had wanted to enter the hospital to visit her sick son. Because visits were not permitted at that hour of the morning and because she kept on insisting, Uncle Ibrahim stood, went over to her, looked at her for a while, and proceeded to beat her up.

When the Glass Shatters

◈ 1 ◈

THE PAPER SELLER SHOUTED, the signal changed, and a black car started off at high speed, almost running over a fat lady wearing a headscarf and causing the lady's husband to get into a violent altercation with the driver. He seemed to see all this through thick, cold glass—the faces of the passersby, the roar of the traffic, the colors of the fluorescent lights on the storefronts all blending into a distant and distorted backdrop. Everything was outside of him. His mind had come to a stop at one particular instant, which it could not get beyond—a frozen instant of horrified realization permeated by clouds and incoherent sounds, just like that experienced by the mind before drowsiness overwhelms it in that brief, infinitely small portion of time that separates waking from sleeping. When he came to himself again, he was crossing Suleiman Pasha Square, it was after eight o'clock, and the shop owners were

136

pulling down over their doors the elongated metal shutters, painted a uniform gray. Cold air struck his face and he started thinking about a place to go. He remembered a small bar on Emad el-Din Street where he used to drink when he was in college and where he wouldn't run into anyone he knew. He turned and walked a few steps in the direction of the bar, but a voice inside his head mocked him, saying that now he looked like a bad actor in a movie by Hasan el-Imam. He slowed his pace and hesitated for a little, but in the end assured himself that he did indeed need a couple of drinks and time to think.

❖ 2 ❖

It was early and the place empty of all but a few customers, who sat at scattered tables. He proceeded quietly to the end of the saloon without looking at any of them so that he wouldn't be obliged to acknowledge them. The lighting was weak, the tablecloth worn and dirty, and the place had an unpleasant smell of damp. The aged Nubian waiter with wrecked teeth smiled politely. The lupine seeds and Pepsi softened the harsh taste of the first, second, and third double brandy, and he was overcome by astonishment. He was possessed by an astonishment that, while genuine, was unlike that ephemeral sensation that he experienced every day. It was, rather, that same feeling of incomprehension that he'd known before only once, when he saw death for the first time. Then, it was his father who was laid out on the bed, covered to the chest with a white sheet, his mouth fastened shut, his eyes closed, and looking as ordinary as though he were sleeping, the only difference being a very slight moroseness of expression, one that was certain to escape notice at first sight and might not even be noticed at all, but which was death itself. He had had the same sensation then as he had now, a feeling that he didn't understand, that he was sad, that suddenly and for no good reason he had been defeated, that his defeat was oppressive, cruel, and final, and that, when the glass shatters, the breaking fragments make a loud noise, then scatter once and for all and are no more.

❖ 3 ❖

He was waiting for her in the cold morning, standing next to the gas station with his hands in the pockets of his overcoat to keep himself warm, staring at the end of the street, where she would appear. She always came late, laughing and apologizing, her short hair bobbing with every step she took. Did anyone else know the reason for that lock of hair, the little one that hung down over her forehead to hide a scar left from an old injury? When they were first married, they had spent days in a cheap boarding house in Alexandria, and she had said to him on the way back, "If our friends ask, we'll say we stayed at the Palestine." He had laughed and answered that rich people didn't visit Alexandria when it was cold like this because they had Luxor and Aswan to go to.

❖ 4 ❖

Those little black intertwined letters had eyes! Real eyes that stared and came alive with joy or clouded over with sorrow and that were now gazing out, hesitantly, anxiously, and with something that swung, with equal force, between mockery and pity.

"My darling Nahid,

"The twentieth of May! Do you remember? My darling, I . . . ."

❖

He couldn't remember now how he'd climbed the stairs or how he got to his apartment, but he remembered clearly finding the lights on in the main room and seeing on the table the dinner she'd made for him and covered with a piece of newspaper (containing the sports section). Then he had gone to the bedroom, opened the door quietly, and turned on the light. She was sleeping and the little boy had curled up snuggled close to her, sticking his head between her arms. He stretched out his hand and shook her, and she woke and smiled when she saw him. He gestured to her to get up, so she did so and followed him outside, walking on tiptoe so as not to wake the child. Then she sat down on the couch in the main room. She was wearing the pink nightdress with the long sleeves and asked him, in a normal tone of voice, though she still hadn't woken up completely, "How are you?"

He said nothing, turned his back, and walked slowly away until he was close to the door of the apartment. Then he came back similarly slowly and said suddenly, looking at the floor, "Nahid, we have to get a divorce."

She looked at him and saw everything in his eyes. Her gaze was fixed and doubtful and a moment went by. Then she said in a steady voice (as though what he had said was something quite ordinary and familiar and happened every day and the only thing that bothered her was that it occurred so often), "What is it this time?"

139

He thrust his hand into his pocket and gave her the letter (doing so immediately and as though he had been waiting for her question, his haste seeming somewhat childish) and she mumbled something as she spread open the folded piece of paper and read it, or pretended to read it, for a few minutes in order to give herself time. Then she pulled herself together, placed the letter calmly on the couch beside her, sighed, and said something to the effect that some sort of misunderstanding had occurred and things weren't the way he thought and he had to give her a chance to explain things in full, after which he could make up his mind. Then she stopped speaking because he had suddenly yelled, in a loud, gasping voice that sounded strange even to him, "You're a prostitute" (or a whore, or something like that, he couldn't remember exactly) and she seized a final opportunity and glared at him and shouted vehemently and angrily, "I will not permit you to . . ."

The first slap silenced her. It struck her head hard, pushing it to one side so that it collided with the dark wooden back of the couch and he slapped her on her face once more and then again, harder. Then he formed a fist and pounded her face and neck and chest and started kicking her naked legs and he didn't stop hitting her until he saw a thin thread of blood trickling from her nose. He looked at her, panting. She wasn't crying and she bowed her head slowly and the blood flowed onto the nightshirt. After a few minutes, she said in a voice that was completely lifeless, "May I go now?"

He didn't answer. He had turned his back on her. A moment later, out of the corner of his eye, he caught sight of her standing up. Then he heard the door of the bedroom close. He didn't remember how many times he made her come back that night—three or maybe four—but each time he would open the door and turn on the light and find her lying next to the child with her eyes closed. He knew she wasn't sleeping but all the same he would shake her as though he was waking her and now it amazed him that he had woken her gently, extending a finger and pressing gently on her back, as though he were waking her for some ordinary purpose on an ordinary night. It amazed him even more that each time she would open her eyes and turn over as though she were waking, and then get up quietly and follow him out of the room. She could have refused or screamed or quarreled with him, or objected or even woken the child, but she didn't do so. Each time she followed him, walking behind him like a small tame animal till she reached the couch and then sitting down and bowing her head. She would say nothing but he would bring his hand down on her again and her body would recoil from the pain and soft stifled moans would issue from her. She wasn't weeping, however. She didn't shed a single tear. She didn't try to shield herself from his hands. She would submit to him totally until he had finished and walked away from her, panting, and then she would withdraw again to the bedroom and he would go in to her again and bring her out and beat her. The last time, when she sat down in front of him, he didn't strike her. He looked at her for a long time and she felt it and raised her head toward him. Her eyes were totally blank, as though she didn't see him. Bruises covered most of her face, blood had caked under her nose, and the small recent cut beneath her eye had started to bleed. He took a step backward, turned around, and moved until he was opposite the closed window. He bent forward suddenly as though examining something on the floor. Then he put one hand on the window handle, flattened the other against the glass, turned his head away, and pursed his lips in an unsuccessful attempt to stop himself from bursting into tears.

Latin and Greek

WANTED, TEACHER OF FRENCH LANGUAGE, for
seven-year-old boy. Salary, LE120 per month. Inter-
view: No. 6, Ghalib St., Mohandessin City, 5–6 p.m.

After half an hour, she had almost given up. One taxi driver
after another went by her with hardly a glance, and a mixture
of boredom, anxiety, and exhaustion seized her. Why did
they refuse to stop? Maybe her white dress looked a bit
standoffish to them. She smiled. She remembered an article
she had read about how people react to things. She waved
once more at an oncoming taxi. This time, she implored the
man with her eyes, an action that for a moment seemed
comical to her, but seemed to have some effect as the driver
stopped right away. "Mohandessin City, driver, please."

When the car moved off, her wristwatch warned that the
hour was approaching six.

After a few minutes, the driver was taking her over University Bridge. She moved her thin body over until she was next to the vehicle's right window. Throngs of students were crossing the bridge in the opposite direction; no doubt they were returning from an evening lecture, or perhaps they'd spent a long time sitting in the cafeteria, as so often happened. She felt like smiling and a feeling of enjoyable sadness was released within her as she recalled days and faces. It was on Saturday, October 18, five years before that she had made her first trip to the university. She still remembered how he had woken her that morning. Papa had gotten everything ready. "I love the funny little things you do," she'd told him.

For the first time since she was a child, he'd wanted to do her hair for her. He stuttered in embarrassment when he asked her, and she laughed and yielded her head to him. She could still remember how he took so long making it look nice that in the end she was compelled, laughing, to do it all over again, while he mumbled an apology. "Goodbye, Professor," he'd said to her in farewell. She turned her back to bring an end to the moment of emotion.

Her father had never gone to university. Poverty had forced him to work from an early age, and he had dreamed for so long of her being awarded her undergraduate degree that it was no surprise when he died a few months before she did so.

A cold gust of air from the outside chilled her. She put out her hand and closed the window tightly. She threw her head back and her dress rustled, reminding her of its owner, a neighbor of hers who loved news and gossip. She started to analyze her feelings at that moment. What did the job mean to her? "One hundred and twenty pounds a month," came back the vehement answer, which was seconded by a quantity of worn-out underwear, socks with holes in them, and an uncountable number of shoes with patched soles. In the same answer, her mother's heartfelt dawn prayers mingled with the heartbroken sobs to which her youngest sister yielded after her first encounter with the sort of men found on public buses. All the money meant to her was to be able to satisfy the needs of those two. She was the only emissary they could dispatch to bring it back. For herself, inside, she cared nothing for banknotes.

One day a girlfriend of hers had told her with genuine sorrow, "Reading has spoiled you." She had laughed then at this odd perspective, even though sometimes it seemed to her that it wasn't so stupid. It wasn't that literature had spoiled her but that it had spoiled the taste of other things for her. It would have been a real pleasure to yearn, like all the other girls, for a villa and a luxury car driven by a colossal husband. There could be no doubt that the speed of the food processor and the whirr of air conditioning bestowed a sort of happiness and that literature had deprived her of that. Inside, she was alone. Alone. One day, on seeing a country wedding procession, she'd almost vomited. Sex was everywhere, from the hashish smoked by the men to the nods and winks of the women, the softness of the thighs, and the eight-year-old girl who started writhing voluptuously when her mother lovingly tied a sash around her hips. Joy was a wild beast with vulgar features, an implacable urge lurking within everyone and everything in creation. Sorrow, however, was transparent and noble as the night. She loved it like winter. It elevated her and lifted her toward itself, and when Beethoven's Ninth surged forward, she would close her eyes and wait for it, and it would come to her as something immortal, like sweet streams purling toward her among the rocks of ignorance and cruelty.

She came to herself to hear the driver saying, "Here's Number 6." A three-story residence of recent date, as evidenced by the piles of sand and stacks of red bricks. Her self-confidence was too feeble to support her at a moment like this but a delicious inner prompting assured her she would get the job, and that she was, simply, very good at French.

"Apartment 15," the doorman told her in a monotone, turning his face away. No doubt there had been lots of girls before her. In the lobby, she found herself face to face with a marble statue of Venus. It was life size. She went up to it. She gazed, her eyes roaming over its noble features, caressing the goddess with the longing of one who had discovered, grown to know, and loved. Even as she was drawn ineluctably toward its splendor, however, she became aware of an uncomfortable feeling that vitiated the beauty. The sacred face seemed strange to her. There was, in the silence of the gods, something with which she was unfamiliar. It seemed to her that there was a certain pinchedness about the goddess's lips—a deep, mysterious, private expression. It was a pain of which gods of smaller size were incapable.

The apartment number was engraved in Roman numerals and a small plaque had been nailed to the wooden door announcing, with all the humility of confidence, "Muhammad Musilhi, Engineer." *Your Excellency Muhammad Bey, ten*

146

years have I sailed literature's seas and I know French well. My mother, for her part, has been ground down standing in the lines of the poor.

She pressed the musical bell. A few moments later and the door opened and, rather than a Nubian servant, a blonde lady appeared, her beauty hinting at a European origin, which was confirmed by her accent when she spoke.

"You've come about the advertisement? Please come this way. I am Madame Musilhi."

With him sat four or five girls, also applicants no doubt. Their features were indistinguishable from one another, the only thing she could make out being the poverty that leered shamelessly from their faces. He, naturally, dominated the gathering, even though he was sitting on the extreme right. He was stout without being excessively so, or, one might say, his body had sufficient fullness to guarantee that he would be addressed by the title "Bey"; never had it occurred to anyone to hail Musilhi Bey by his name alone, or even accompanied by any other than this, his preferred, title—as though someone were to say to him, "Mr. Musilhi" or "Engineer Musilhi." No one would dare to do that, neither colleague nor stranger.

In reality, this phenomenon was not so much related to his stoutness or to the smartness of his clothes, or even to the affection people bore him, as to his being a strong man well versed in the uses of power and an expert in the arts of command with a commanding look and a reassuringly regal way of moving. He even made an effort to reduce the movements of his hands, while adding to them a decisive slowness. As for his tone of voice, any tremor had disappeared from it

147

years ago. Indeed, Musilhi Bey was a strong man in every way. Even his shoes were shiny and radiant. "Work! Work!" he would repeat, and "In this world, weakness and extinction have the same meaning." Musilhi Bey had quickly removed himself from the lanes of the Sayeda Zeinab quarter, where he had grown up, to Mohandessin, but, despite his sudden wealth, he was neither thief nor conman. Rather, once he had obtained his secondary school certificate, he had refused to go to university. What was the value of study? He preferred to work in the import-export business—a legitimate profession acknowledged by the laws of the state. Musilhi Bey was a realist. He had grasped from the start that changing the existing order had for centuries been the dream of poets and of the heroes of history books, and should, therefore, be left to them. For the sake of change, heroes had been imprisoned and thrown onto the street. He, however, was not a hero and didn't want to be one. He had no time to be a hero. How long would he live? At the best estimate, another thirty years. He would, therefore, live to enjoy life, and to work. Better, then, to fight the good fight for Musilhi and leave things as they were, or let them change, or let them be as they would; his intelligence would be employed in the service of his own sacred interests.

This was how Musilhi Bey had succeeded and become rich, and then even richer, and each night he was accustomed to lie down next to his beautiful wife of Swiss manufacture and read a little in the biographies of heroes and leaders—of those tortured by impossible ideas, the history of the idiots. Today, Musilhi Bey was announcing in the newspapers that he needed a woman to teach his son French, and there was great competition, and he sat among them, examining and testing, so that he could select the worthiest among them with confidence. A mocking memory returned him to the dark room in one of the private Qur'an schools for small children in Sayeda Zeinab where he had received his first lessons. "It's all about money, Musilhi," he thought to himself. Now this girl with the white dress was sitting in front of him, gentle as a breeze and so modest he almost felt pity for her. But Musilhi Bey hated weakness and emotion.

"Name in full."

"Nadia Abd el-Salam."

"Degree."

"Graduate, Humanities, Cairo University."

The embarrassing words died on her lips. It was that feeling of mortification. She had to look him in the face. She decided to smile. She failed.

"You graduated from the French Department." He said the words as though stating a fact.

"No. I did Latin and Greek."

A few silent seconds, which felt like an eternity, followed.

"But in the advertisement I said a French teacher." He said the words with a friendliness that underscored his command of the situation.

She had to get her voice out somehow.

"I studied French at a private institute for five years."

"Your identification, if you please."

She handed him her ID card. His face took on an expression of indifference. Out of the corner of her eye she noticed one of the girls whispering laughingly to her neighbor.

"My dear Miss Nadia, I'd like to make something quite

clear. My son is not in need of someone to teach him the elements of French. He speaks it fluently. He needs someone to go over his lessons from the Lycée Français with him."

"My French is very good."

"Well, we'll see. Kareem!" he called out, looking around him. A blond young boy emerged and went up to his father.

"This is Mademoiselle Nadia. She's your new teacher. Shake hands with her and say something to her in French."

"Okay. Are you my new teacher?"

Her French really was very good.

"Papa, she doesn't say anything."

Musilhi Bey, who had been listening closely, pretended to be busy reading his papers, and when he raised his head, Nadia was getting up to go.

An Old Blue Dress
and A Close-fitting Covering
for the Head, Brightly Colored

An Old Blue Dress

As soon as I got to know her, I took her to dinner at a small restaurant in Opera Square and the next week I took her to the cinema. Afterward I drove her home and before she got out of the car, I asked her to come and visit me at my flat. She showed no surprise or shock and she didn't make a show of being angry the way women do. She just gave me a mysterious look, then asked quietly for the address and enquired about the doorkeeper and the neighbors. She was on time for the appointment.

I'd prepared myself with a couple of drinks and sat next to her in the reception room, paving the way with a long bright conversation. I was expecting all the kinds of resistance and coquetry that normally take place on a woman's first visit but when the critical moment came, she made no objection

151

and surrendered to my kisses. Then, begging my pardon in a whisper, she started removing her clothes one by one and hanging them carefully on the hanger, as though playing a part or fulfilling an agreement. When we'd finished, she moved her naked body away from me and, lying on her back, joined her hands together beneath her head and stared at the ceiling. At that moment she seemed utterly sad and, being an expert in the melancholy moods that follow the spending of passion, I stretched out my hand and toyed with a lock of her dishevelled hair. She patted my hand and said, "You know what? Sometimes a girl can feel really sorry for herself."

I put my arm around her and whispered, "Never mind," as I embarked on a new kiss.

She was sweet-natured and poor, and she told me about her father who was a driver and her five brothers and sisters and their room on the roof in el-Mawardi Street, and her Saudi husband who had disappeared after two months. And she laughed as she imitated the accent of the consular official and described to me his luxury flat in Zamalek.

I can see her now.

I see her hair, wet after a shower, after she had put on my patterned silk dressing gown, rolling up the sleeves to accommodate her slight build, and I see her in the evening at the moment before leaving my flat, alone in the dark entryway, where she would stand as though taking off the face of the lover and replacing it with an ordinary face like those of the passersby, then carefully open the door and leave, her footfall reaching my ears and growing louder as it receded. And I see her spending a whole day with me going around the shops to pick me out clothes to her own taste, examining and comparing everything carefully, as though we were really married and she my beloved, thrifty, wife.

Then I see her for the last time that morning. We had arranged to meet at the bus stop next to her house. It was cold, and the people standing at the stop had taken refuge in a solitary spot of sunlight on the pavement, where she too stood, in her old blue winter dress that was a little threadbare at the elbows. Her face seemed to me changed and strange, and when she sat down next to me in the car, I felt as though something oppressive had imposed itself between us.

She was the first to speak. She said, "The hospital's at the end of Salah Salim Road."

I headed the car in that direction and started in on a new act of the play. Sighing as though my patience was exhausted, I said, "I told you, I can marry you."

I'd said the same words a hundred times over the past two days but she'd made no comment, not even once. Whenever I offered to marry her, she'd wait until I'd finished and then go on with what she'd been saying about the operation as though I hadn't spoken. She knew that I'd never marry her and I somewhat over-insisted so that it would be plain to her that I wasn't serious.

The hospital was a small white building with a large sign that said Adeeb Maternity Home and it seemed to me—as she went up the marble stairs with slow uncertain steps and bowed head—it seemed to me that I was in some film, playing the role of the warder who leads the erring woman to her inescapable doom.

We met Dr. Adeeb, with his flabby body, broad bald patch and soft, full face, in his office, where he welcomed us

153

tersely. Then he asked me, with a show of innocence, "Are you married?"

I nodded, and he said, "Why do you want to have the operation?"

I replied—as she had instructed me—, "The fact is we have two children . . . and we're quite happy that way."

With the formalities thus disposed of, the doctor's face took on a resolute expression and he told us, in his normal voice this time, "The operation costs five-hundred pounds and the anaesthetic's a hundred."

I'd got the money ready in an envelope and gave it to the doctor, with thanks. No sooner had he put it in a drawer than he leaped up and said, "So let's be getting on with things. This way, madam."

The doctor led the way and we—she, the nurse, and I—had to go down a long dark corridor to reach the operating theater with its double doors and twin glass portholes. We walked in silence. Then there, right at the door, she suddenly turned toward me and whispered, "I'm very scared, Salah." But I didn't say a word. I stayed rooted to the spot until the nurse pulled her inside by the hand, the door swinging violently behind her. I had a headache and as I sat in the hallway I thought that it was a difficult situation but I couldn't marry her however sweet she was and however much I loved her. She was—when you came right down to it—simply a fallen woman. And also, mightn't it be that she'd got pregnant deliberately so as to trap me into marriage? Wasn't that a real possibility?

◈ 2 ◈

A Close-fitting Covering for the Head, Brightly Colored

What I liked about her most were her morals, which were impeccable. There were five of us in the accountancy class and she was the only female student who covered her hair. Her head scarf wasn't one of those flowing, billowy ones; it was just a cover for the head, a round piece of embroidered silk to cover her hair of a sort that I found out later was called a *bonnet*; she had a varied collection of *bonnet*s, each dress having its own of the same color. And her beauty was stunning: wide black eyes, a complexion of shining, angelic whiteness, a little nose as delicate as some delicious fruit, and full lips, which, when slightly parted, revealed regular, pearly teeth.

All that beauty, and swathed in a grave and modest comportment that commanded respect. No frivolous laugh escaped her lips and there wasn't a wanton or uncalled for word to any of her male colleagues or a single attempt to attract attention to herself. In addition she was so profoundly religious that she would ask the teacher to halt the class so that she wouldn't have to skip the afternoon prayer. I was attracted to her, but despite all my experience with women I didn't dare. How could I pollute the surface of that dignified bearing with a cheap flirtatious word? Months passed as I watched her in silence during class; and, as I knew for sure from the slight quiver that would pass over her lovely face whenever our eyes met, she could feel my glances.

One evening, the telephone rang at home and I heard her voice on the line—smooth and drowsy, as though she was asleep or had just woken up. She asked me about some point that was unclear in the last class, then thanked me and hung up. I stayed awake the whole night thinking. Why had she called me specifically? First, I was weak at accounting, as she well knew, and second she had the number of the teacher himself and could have asked him if she'd wanted. Could it be that . . . ?

The idea that she might love me had me soaring like a bird in the sky.

I rang her the next day and her mother enquired coldly, "Who is this?"

"Her classmate Salah, *Tante*," I answered quickly.

She said nothing for a moment as though carefully weighing the situation. Then she called her. This time we talked for ages. I discovered that she had two sisters and that her father was a university professor who worked in the Gulf and I told her about my father who had died recently and complained of the complicated inheritance procedures. In the end, I asked her if I could ring her from time to time. She laughed and said, "Why not? That way we can encourage each other to study."

Our phone conversations became long, daily affairs that strengthened the love in my heart until one day my feelings overflowed and I suddenly said to her, "Listen. I love you. Will you marry me?"

She said nothing for a long time. Then she responded, in a voice that sounded to me low and sad, that this was what she'd been afraid of at the beginning and that, though I was as outstanding a young man as any girl could wish for, she wasn't thinking of marriage yet. It was a hard blow, and I asked her in a despairing voice if that meant that she was refusing me. She replied that she was neither accepting me nor refusing me; she just wasn't thinking about marriage. Our calls continued and I didn't talk to her about marriage after that, but I would express my love every day, telling her, "I love you, I love you." Sometimes she'd laugh and sometimes she'd say, "If you really love me, study hard." One day, when the finals were approaching, she told me, "Why don't we review together? Come to the house tomorrow. I've told Mummy and Daddy."

I spent the night as in a fabulous dream. I didn't sleep and I didn't read a word, and when the appointed time came, I was wearing my best clothes with my hair neatly brushed and my face shaved. How happy I felt as I rang their melodious doorbell!

Her house was lovely and her family lovelier still. Her father was a man of great distinction who embraced me in his fatherliness, and her mother, still beautiful despite her age, covered her hair with a somber black *bonnet*. I really liked it about her parents that they would leave us alone in the study and close the door on us. Didn't that demonstrate the trust they had in their daughter, and in my own morals too?

How beautiful love is! I started going to see her every day. I'd sit beside her as we went over our lessons and talked, and I'd move close to her and smell the scent of her hair and suddenly surprise her by grasping her soft, plump hand, feeling it melt in my grip. At such moments, she'd color and gasp and whisper fearfully, "Are you mad? If Mummy caught us it'd be a disaster."

157

Then one day, when I'd gone to review with her as usual and had sat down at the desk and spread the lecture notes out in front of me, she informed me, casually, that her parents had gone out and that they wouldn't be back before evening. The moment this sunk in, I felt the blood seethe in my body and a veil fell over my eyes, so that I couldn't make out what I was seeing. In a strangled voice, I asked her to bring me a glass of water and the moment she got up and turned around I grasped her arm and pulled her toward me, covering her face and neck with hot kisses. She let out a low scream and resisted a little, then surrendered to my embrace, and we dissolved in a long, burning kiss sweeter than any I'd tasted in my life before. When I recovered my senses, I found her face had turned pale and was wet with tears, and it wasn't long before she broke into a bout of painful weeping. I tried to calm her and said I was sorry I hadn't been able to control myself. I told her, to make light of the matter, that it was only a kiss after all, but my darling screamed in my face, "It's nothing to you, but for me it's a catastrophe. Me, on whom no man but my father has ever laid a hand—how could I have allowed you to kiss me? What am I going to tell my father? What am I going to tell my mother?" My beloved collapsed in a new fit of weeping and wailing and I couldn't stand it, so I left in a hurry feeling extremely upset.

Then there we were, my mother and I, in their living room with my beloved seated like a shining star between her parents, wearing a bright red dress with a *bonnet* of the same color. My mother spoke at length about my upbringing and my morals and the wealth my father had left me and how much she wanted to see me happily married. When the talk turned to the bridal settlement and the jewelry, my beloved stretched out her beautiful, delicate hand, adjusted the *bonnet*, which had slipped a little, and said to my mother in her magical, dulcet voice that the sum of twenty thousand pounds wasn't nearly enough, and spoke of young women related to her whose settlements had reached as much as sixty or even seventy thousand. Then she ended by saying, politely but firmly, that she couldn't possibly accept less than thirty.

And I nudged my mother eagerly to agree.

Izzat Amin Iskandar

IZZAT AMIN ISKANDAR was my classmate in First Preparatory. He was on the short side, his body strong and broad, his head large, his hair black and smooth. He wore glasses, along with a slight meek smile, almost of supplication, and that Coptic look—sometimes shifty, misgiving, and frightened, sometimes profound, submissive, and burdened with guilt and distress. He also had an artificial leg and a crutch. The crutch ended in a piece of rubber that prevented it from making a noise or slipping, and his artificial leg he covered with his school pants and a sock and shoe to make it look normal.

Each morning Izzat limped into the classroom leaning on his crutch, dragging his artificial leg and swinging from one side to the other with every step until he reached the end of his bench. There, in the corner next to the window, he would sit down and lay his crutch on the ground, paying it no further attention. He would completely absorb himself in the lesson, writing down carefully everything that the teacher said, listening alertly and knitting his brow in concentration and then raising his hand with a question—as though by becoming so involved in the lesson he could insinuate himself into the throng, hide himself in our midst, and become, for a few hours, just one student among the others, stigmatized by neither crutch nor limp.

When the bell sounded for break, the moment its splendid tones rang out, the students would all cheer for joy, throw down whatever they were holding, and push and shove their way, sometimes even knocking one another over, to the door of the classroom, from where they descended to the playground. Only Izzat Amin Iskandar would receive the sound as though it was the fulfillment of some ancient, awaited prophecy, close his exercise book, bend quietly down, and then take the sandwich and the comic from his bag and spend the break seated where he was, reading and eating. If any of the other students were to look at him and show any curiosity or pity, Izzat would smile broadly while continuing to read, to make it clear how much he was enjoying himself, as though it was the pleasure of reading and that alone that kept him from going down to the playground.

◈

It was the first time I'd taken my bike to school. It was a Thursday afternoon and the playground was empty of all but a few students playing soccer on the far side. I started riding my bike. I would cross the playground back and forth, making circles round the trees, imagining myself in a bike race and yelling at the top of my lungs, "Ladies and gentlemen, and now for the World Cycling Championship!" In my mind's eye, I could see the public, the important people, and the riders with whom I was competing and hear the shouts and whistles of the fans. I was always in first place, reaching the finishing line before the others and receiving bunches of flowers and kisses of congratulation.

I continued to play like this for some time and then suddenly I got a feeling that I was being observed. I turned and saw Izzat Amin Iskandar sitting on the laboratory steps. He'd been watching me from the beginning and when our eyes met he smiled and waved, so I set off toward him and he started his standing up process, leaning on one hand against the wall of the steps and grasping his crutch under his arm; then he raised his body slowly until he was upright and came down the steps one by one. When he reached me, he started examining the bicycle closely. He took hold of the handle bar, rang the bell a number of times, and then bent and ran his fingers over the spokes of the front wheel, muttering in a low voice, "Nice bike."

I was quick to say with pride, "It's a Raleigh 24, racing wheels, three-speed."

He gave the bike another look over, as though to test the truth of what I'd said, then asked, "Do you know how to ride with your hands in the air?"

I nodded and set off on the bike. I was an expert rider and happy to show off in front of him. I pedaled hard until I got to top speed and could feel the bike shaking beneath me. Then I raised my hands carefully from the handlebar, until my arms were straight up in the air. I stayed that way for a bit, then turned, and came back to where he'd taken a few steps forward to the middle of the playground. Coming to a halt in front of him, I said as I got off, "Happy now?"

He didn't answer me, but bent his head and started looking at the bike as though weighing something profound and surprising in his mind. He struck the ground with his crutch and moved forward a step until he was up against the bike. Then he grasped the handlebar in his hand, bent toward me, and whispered, "Let me have a ride, please" and went on insistently repeating, "Please, please."

I didn't take in what he was saying and stared at him. At that moment he looked like someone swept by a wave of such longing that he couldn't stop himself or go back, and when he found I didn't reply he started shaking the handle bar violently and shouting, in anger this time, "I said give me a ride!" Then he tried to jump up and get on and we both lost our balance and almost fell over.

I don't remember what I was thinking right then but something propelled me toward him and I found myself helping him onto the bike. He leaned his weight on my shoulder and the crutch and after several strenuous attempts was able to raise his body up high and then get his sound leg over to the other side of the bike and sit on the saddle. His plan was to hold his artificial leg out in front to avoid the pedal and at the same time to push the other pedal hard with his sound leg. This was extremely difficult but, in the end, possible. Izzat settled himself on the bike and with my hand on his back I started to push him forward gently and carefully, and when the bike started to move and he began pedaling, I let go. He lost his balance and wobbled violently but quickly recovered his poise, straightened out, and started to control the bike. He had to make a huge effort to pedal with one leg while keeping his balance but moments passed and the bike proceeded slowly and Izzat passed first the big tree and then the canteen kiosk and I found myself clapping and shouting, "Well done, Izzat!"

He kept going in a straight line until he had almost reached the end of the playground where he had to make a turn, which scared me. But he made the turn carefully and skillfully and when he came back the other way he seemed confident and in complete control of the bike—so much so that he changed gear once, and then again, until the rushing air made his hair fly.

The bicycle was charging ahead at great speed now and Izzat passed down the pathway that extended between the trees, his form appearing and disappearing amid the criss-crossing foliage. He'd done it, and I watched him as he leaned back on the bike, which was flying like an arrow now, raised his head, and let out a long, loud cry that echoed around the playground—a strange, drawn-out, cracked cry that sounded as though it had been long imprisoned within his chest. He was shouting, "See! Seeeeeeeeeee!"

❖

A little later, when I ran over to him, the bike was on its side on the ground, the front wheel still spinning and whirring, and the dull-colored artificial leg, with its sock, shoe, and dark, hollow inside, lying separated from his body at a distance, looking as though it had just been cut off or was a separate creature with its own independent life. Izzat was lying face down, his hand on the place were the leg had been amputated and which had started to bleed and make a stain that was spreading over his ripped pants. I called to him and he slowly raised his head. There were cuts on his forehead and lips and his face looked strange to me without the glasses. He gazed at me for a moment as though gathering his wits, then said in a weak voice, with the ghost of a smile, "Did you see me ride the bike?"

Dearest Sister Makarim

IN THE NAME OF GOD, the Merciful, the Compassionate, from whom we seek help, and praise and blessing upon Our Prophet Muhammad, Lord of All Mankind, and upon his kin and companions, one and all.

To continue:

Dearest sister Makarim,

We long so very much to see you, my dear sister. I swear, my dear Makarim, our thoughts are with you always and just yesterday I woke with a terrible start in the middle of the night to the sound of someone weeping—it was your sister-in-law Batta. She was awake and crying hard and she said to me, "Hasan, I just can't bear the thought of Makarim all on her own over there with Mum."

Our hearts are with you, dear sister, and all of us—me, Batta, and the children—pray to God, Mighty and Glorious, that He inspire you with patience and steady your heart. You have proved yourself, my dear Makarim, a true daughter, and anyone who knows what you've done for our mother in her illness can testify to that. You must know, my dear sister, that your care of our mother will not go unrewarded, for a single prayer from our beloved mother will open wide to you the gates of Paradise, God willing.

My beloved sister, I have shown our mother's x-rays and tests to the doctors here and they all confirm that the growth—and I'm so sorry to have to tell you this—is in the tertiary stage, meaning that surgery will not help and the only solution is chemotherapy. Makarim, you are a Believer and have been raised to obey God and submit to His decree and you know, dear sister, that sickness and health, life and death, are in the hands of the Creator, Glorious and Sublime, and that the children of Adam have no say in them.

I imagine, my dear sister, that you would like to know of my welfare. I swear to God, my dear Makarim, that the last thing I'd wish to do is add to your worries. You have enough to deal with. Since Batta and I got back from our last pilgrimage we've had nothing but troubles, praise God for all things. Last month, I felt a terrible pain in my right side and it got so bad at night that I fell out of bed onto the floor, weeping like a child. They did tests at the hospital and the doctor told me my left kidney had huge stones in it and they'd have to do an operation. To cut a long story short, my dear sister, I had the operation and they kept me in the hospital for three weeks. I swear by the Almighty, my dear sister Makarim, the whole thing—operation, tests, and all the rest—cost me ten thousand riyals and not a penny less, praise be to God for all things. And then, as soon as I'd got over the operation I had a problem with my sponsor, who's the owner of the school where Batta and I work.* He's one of the important sheikhs and very well connected and he could have us thrown out of the country in twenty-four hours if he wanted. The problem is that my sponsor discovered that I frequently visit the villa of Sheikh Fahd al-Rubay'i and sometimes give his children help with their lessons, so he thinks I'm giving them private tutoring for money even though I assured him that Sheikh Fahd and I are just friends in God and basically we meet to study the Qur'an together. But the sponsor wasn't convinced and he doesn't miss a chance to hint to me that I'm giving private lessons. I got so mad that two days ago I yelled in his face, "Fear God, Sheikh! The burden of proof is on the accuser, Sheikh! Shame on you for accusing me with no proof!" But it made no difference, my dear sister, and he has docked me two months' incentives, God forgive him.

What can I say, my dear Makarim? I swear to God that Batta and I are thinking seriously about coming back to Egypt once and for all. Ten years away from home and every penny we make we spend as soon as it comes to us—in other words we're "as poor as the day you made us, O Lord!" praise be to God. And what makes us really angry is that people in Egypt think we're living in the lap of luxury and laying aside a fortune.

To end with, my dear sister, I want you to put our minds at rest with all the latest news concerning our dear mother

---

* *The riyal is the unit of currency in Saudi Arabia. Foreigners can only work in Saudi Arabia at the recognizance of a Saudi citizen, who retains their passport and controls their movements in and out of the country. Sponsors typically also take a percentage of the worker's earnings.*

the moment it happens, and to tell her, my dear Makarim, that if it weren't for our present very difficult circumstances, I would have given up everything and come with Batta and the children to stay by her side, for all our bounties and blessings are from her. I would also like you, my dear sister, to read over her the Prayer of the Distressed, in emulation of the Prophet, peace and blessings be upon him (please try to make a ritual ablution first). The Prayer goes, "O God, I beg of Your mercy that You leave me not to the devices of my own soul, even for the blinking of an eye, but ameliorate my state in all things, for there is no god but You."

If you say this often enough, my dear Makarim, you will discover great bounty, God willing. Concerning the amount you requested to move my mother to a private hospital, were I to spend all the money in the world and sell the clothes from off my back for the sake of my mother, I could not repay that wonderful woman the half of what she has done for us. Most unfortunately, however, my financial circumstances are extremely difficult and do not permit me to comply—so much so that I have had to borrow money from one of my good friends here to get through the month.

Anyway, I consulted Dr. Husni Abid about private hospitals and he said that the treatment in the government hospitals is just the same that they give in the private hospitals and the only difference is that the private hospitals demand extortionate fees, medicine in Egypt having become an entirely commercial affair, God forbid. This is the opinion of Dr. Husni, who is a well-known doctor here and a good man who fears the Lord (over Whom we give precedence to none), and all thanks to you, my beloved sister.

My dear Makarim, please—with this, you'll find another small envelope addressed to the real estate broker Hagg Gharib. Go find him at the Amana Café and give it to him immediately and tell him to contact me by telephone urgently. If he can't get hold of me, he should call Sheikh Fahd al-Rubay'i, telephone no. (06) 582–1465. The matter is most important and urgent, my dear Makarim. May God reward you well, my beloved sister.

Peace be upon you, and the mercy of God and His blessings.

Your brother,
Hasan Muhammad Nagati
Al-Qasim, Muharram 5, 1413
[True copy]

The Sorrows of Hagg Ahmad

HAGG AHMAD RETURNED HOME after praying the extra Ramadan prayers in the mosque and sat and watched television until his wife, Hagga Dawlat, called him to have his predawn meal. Hagg Ahmad got up slowly, sat down at the table, rolled up the sleeves of his gallabiya, pronounced the formula "In the Name of God, the Merciful, the Compassionate," and started. First of all he drank a glass of warm lime juice, designed to act both as a disinfectant for the digestive system and as wake-up call for the stomach so that the food did not catch it offguard. At the same moment, the Filipina maid was going down the corridor carrying a tray of food to the room of Hagg Azzam, Hagg Ahmad's aged father, who had been living with them for two years.

Hagg Ahmad stretched out his hand and tore off a large mouthful of the hot, mud-oven-baked, flaky pastry swimming in butter and dipped it into the dish of beans that sat right next to it on the table. The beans had passed through many stages of preparation, including being slowly stewed, then released from their skins, then mashed and mixed with slices of tomato, and, finally, being garnished with just the right amount of corn oil, lime, pepper, and cumin, turning them into a thing of delight for those who ate them and a fortification for them against the long day's fasting ahead. Hagg Ahmad half closed his eyes in relish and started chewing slowly, like a virtuoso warming up his instrument with a few simple melodies before launching it into the world of the symphony.

"God bless you, Hagga," murmured Hagg Ahmed warmly, masticating.

"And good health to you, Hagg," replied his wife in a gratified tone.

After the beans, Hagg Ahmed had made up his mind to move on to the parsley omelet situated to his right, to be followed by a glass of chilled hibiscus from Aswan, after which there might still be room for a few boiled eggs, which Hagg Ahmad would eat as is, without bread, lest he satisfy his appetite completely and thus be denied the sweet, which he had it on good authority tonight would be dishes of rice pudding on whose firm, milky, surface gratings of delicious coconut had been sprinkled.

However, no sooner had Hagg Ahmad stretched out his hand for a little more of the flaky pastry than an agonized high-pitched cry resounded, cleaving the calm of the night, and pandemonium broke out. Hagga Dawlat leaped up in terror, her chair falling over backward with a loud clatter, and Hagg Ahmad hurried after her as fast as his obesity and rheumatism would allow. The Filipina maid was standing at the door to Hagg Azzam's room, her Asiatic face clothed in an awful fear, and the room was filled with a heavy silence. To Hagg Ahmad, as he entered, it seemed that a foul, earthy smell filled his nose and he saw his father stretched out on the bed, his toothless mouth open and his eyes staring into emptiness, while on his aged face a fixed expression had taken hold, as though he had been taken mightily by surprise, once and for eternity.

Hagg Azzam was dead, and Dawlat let out a long wail to announce the painful news, while Hagg Ahmad threw his heavy body onto his father's corpse and buried his face in his bosom, bursting into tears like a lost child. He was totally absorbed, and when a few moments later he returned to his senses the room was empty, so he stood, wiped away his tears with his sleeve and recited the opening chapter of the Qur'an. Then he closed his father's eyelids and mouth, covered his head with the sheet, and inserted his hand gently under the pillow, where he took hold of the keys, which he placed in his pocket. Next he went out to the telephone, to announce the news of the passing of the dear departed to his relatives and acquaintances.

An hour later, Hagg Ahmad, having donned his navy blue safari suit, was seated in the midst of the mourners in the drawing room as the Filipina circulated among those present with a tray of coffee and cold water. The neighbors came first, then Mr. Sa'id Azzam (the deceased's middle son and an undersecretary at the Ministry of Irrigation) his face pale and eyes bemused at the sudden shock. When Adil (the youngest son, who worked for American Express) arrived, he screamed and insisted on seeing his father and when they pulled the sheet back for him, he fell rigid to the floor, so they carried him into the parlor and rubbed his face with cologne. Mrs. Amna (the deceased's only daughter) flung herself into the apartment and the moment Hagga Dawlat caught sight of her, she screamed in a choking voice fit to break your heart, "Come and see, Amna! Our father's dead, Amna!" to which Amna responded by slapping herself violently on the cheeks, during which operation she collapsed onto the floor of the corridor, and Hagg Ahmad left the mourners and hurried over to the two grief-stricken women to calm them down. Then he took his brother Adil, who had become somewhat quieter, to one side and gave him a bundle containing one thousand pounds and agreed with him on the arrangements for the next day—the undertaker, the tent, the death announcement, and the rest.

Hagg Ahmad was accustomed to dealing with calamities. He was the eldest of his brothers and his work as a construction contractor had gained him common sense and sound nerves, which were further strengthened by his deep faith and knowledge of matters of religion. See him now, sitting among the mourners, silent and, head bowed, his face showing how both sad he is and also how he clings to the patience in adversity that befits the true believer. Unlike the others, Hagg Ahmad neither cries nor goes into convulsions, but his sorrows weigh upon his heart like a mountain, his looks are downcast and broken-hearted, and his lips mutter verses from the Book in the hope of alleviating the pain. It would be fitting tonight were Hagg Ahmad to keep thoughts of his father ever in the forefront of his mind, remembering how his father had looked after him and his younger brothers, sacrificing for them his comfort and his money, and how, having acquitted this sacred task in full, he was now about to go to his Lord. "*O soul at peace, return thou unto thy Lord, well-pleased, well-pleasing!* Verily, God has spoken truly!" murmured Hagg Ahmad as he sat amid the mourners in the drawing room lost in thought and prayer for his departed father. Then, at a certain moment, he raised his head to crack and stretch his neck (a meaningless, normal action, just like someone playing with the strap of his watch or twisting his mustache between two fingers while talking). However that may be, Hagg Ahmad's eyes, when he raised his head, fell on the clock on the wall. The large golden hands pointed to half past three in the morning, and when Hagg Ahmad once more bowed his head, something in his chest had changed, something ignoble had started to prick him like a small, bothersome needle. Hagg Ahmad tried to resume his meditations on the departed but it was no use. The pricks merged and coalesced and an unworthy thought started to pursue him and weigh upon his mind: he hadn't yet had his predawn meal. The calamity had struck before he'd had time to eat more than a single mouthful, there was only a quarter of an hour left to go before the dawn prayer, and his hollow stomach was nipping at him. He was hungry and wanted to eat and that was all there was to it.

When things came to this pass, Hagg Ahmad felt embarrassed, even ashamed. He despised himself. "You want," he thought to himself, "to eat, fill your belly, and belch, with your father only an hour dead? Can't you put up with being hungry for one day, out of respect for the one who raised you and made you a man of means? The souls of the dead see and hear, and your father's soul may this very minute be smiling sadly and despising your ingratitude. So soon does your mind turn aside from this calamity in favor of an omelet, and beans with tomatoes?" Hagg Ahmad uttered the words "I seek refuge with God" in an audible voice and twisted his head sharply to the right, as though to expel the evil thought, but Satan—God curse him—is a clever foe. See how he whispers to him, in calm, convincing tones, "Why all the fuss? Has the predawn meal suddenly become something reprehensible, or forbidden in religion?" He knew himself too well to think that he could tolerate the day's fast without a meal before dawn. If he didn't eat now, he would break his fast tomorrow, and what ignominy that would bring down on him! So he should eat, because tomorrow was going to be a hard day. He had to attend to the washing, shrouding, and burial of the corpse plus the funeral and a million other headaches. How could he get through it all on an empty stomach? And then there were all these people seated around him in mourning only a few minutes before the canon was due to sound to mark the start of the feast. How was he to know they hadn't eaten at home? If they were as hungry as he was, they wouldn't look so peaceful! Of course they'd all eaten well at home before coming to weep their bitter tears over the dear departed. He himself, if his father had died somewhere other than in his own home, would have eaten and drunk before going to pay his respects. It was perfectly natural, and there was nothing reprehensible or forbidden about it.

Thus did Hagg Ahmad's resistance erode, until, at forty minutes past three, it was gone altogether. There were five minutes left and Hagg Ahmad jumped up like someone who's just remembered something important and trotted out of the drawing room muttering words of apology. He hastened his pace as he crossed the small corridor that led to the kitchen and there he found his wife, Hagga Dawlat, standing in silence and doing nothing, as though she was waiting for him, as though the long years of cohabitation had made her expect his appearance in the kitchen at that very moment. Dawlat gave him a look of understanding. Her eyes were swollen from crying and she had slapped herself so hard there were dark marks on her cheeks. In a voice whose sorrow and tremulousness she worked hard to maintain, she said, "Shall I get you a pot of yogurt, Hagg?"

Despite all her precautions, her voice and posture, and the way the dim light emanated from the kitchen, gave Hagg Ahmad the feeling that they were somehow conspirators and he shouted in her face, "Yogurt? What damn yogurt? What's that got to do with anything?"

Dawlat bowed her head as though shamed and quietly withdrew across the corridor. When she had disappeared completely, Hagg Ahmad stepped inside the kitchen and closed the door gently but firmly behind him. And there, on the marble counter next to the sink, Hagg Ahmad saw the dish of beans with tomatoes of which he'd been able to eat only one mouthful.

Waiting for the Leader

"MY BROTHERS, the twenty-third of August will remain forever engraved on our hearts in letters of light. Twenty-five years ago to this day, el-Nahhas Pasha, leader of the Wafd and of the nation, departed from us, his pure spirit calling down curses on the oppressors as it ascended.* That day, my brothers, the tyrant Abdel Nasser refused to let us accompany our leader to his place of rest and yet we went out onto the streets. We went out onto the streets and Egypt, to her last man and woman, went out with us to bid farewell to her devoted son, after which Abdel Nasser's prisons received us and we entered them content, reconciled to our fate, for we—sons of the Mighty Wafd—will remain faithful to the Covenant so long as there is breath in our bodies."

---

* The Wafd was Egypt's leading political party in the first half of the twentieth century. The party and its leader, Mustafa el-Nahhas (1879–1965), were banned from political activity following the 1952 Revolution, but the party was allowed to resume its activities in 1983.

Kamil el-Zahhar was standing on the dais and now that his passion was ignited his voice reverberated around the hall and he started punching the air with his fist. Behind him, a life-size portrait in oils of the Leader, Mustafa el-Nahhas, could be seen on the wall and next to him sat those two pillars of the Wafd, Muhammad Bey Bassiouni (may God prolong his life), former director of Mustafa el-Nahhas's office (a venerable seventy-five years old, sick of body and weak of sight, yet with a heart still overflowing with love for the Wafd and its leader) and, on his left, with his countryman's cloak and towering figure, Sheikh Ali Sahhab, the well-known Wafdist member of parliament and fellow townsman of el-Nahhas Pasha, from Samannud, in the province of el-Gharbiya. The celebration in memory of el-Nahhas was taking place in the living room of the home of Kamil el-Zahhar in el-Mounira and the room was crowded to capacity, some of those in attendance even having to follow events from outside. They were a mixture of neighbors, a few passersby who had come up out of curiosity, and, and these were the majority, the poor of the area—men and women dragging children along with them, their clothes shabby and dirty, the penetrating smell of their sweat combining with the exhaled breath of the audience and the cigarette smoke so that the air in the room was now oppressively offensive and stifling. El-Zahhar brought his speech to a close and sat down, pouring with sweat, to thunderous applause, and it was the turn of Muhammad Bey Bassiouni (God grant him health and strength). Rising from his seat with the assistance of Bora'i, his private driver, he advanced slowly to the microphone, swept the audience with his eyes for a moment, and said, "I want to ask you, brothers, why we have come here tonight. Have we come seeking wealth or positions? Certainly not! We have gathered here for him, for Mustafa el-Nahhas. We have come to reawaken his sainted memory. Mustafa el-Nahhas, you live on! You will remain in Egypt's heart so long as the Nile runs and the pyramids stand. Mustafa el-Nahhas . . . ." Here, Bassiouni Bey suddenly stopped and bent his head in silence. A fugitive tear escaped from behind his thick glasses and all of a sudden his aged body shook and he burst into violent weeping. An embarrassed silence reigned in the room, but Sheikh Ali Sahhab's excitement took fire and he leaped to his feet and shouted three times, in his deep voice, "No leader after el-Nahhas!"

The people repeated the call behind him but Kamil seemed to sense that the listeners had tired of the heat, the crush, and the constant clapping and cheering and he went to the microphone and thanked them, and read the opening chapter of the Qur'an with them for the repose of the leader's soul. Then the two pillars of the Wafd departed along with some of the rest. The majority, however, stayed in the room; they had attended el-Zahhar's celebrations before and knew the routine. They crowded, therefore, in front of the dais next to a small, closed side door. A moment later, this opened, and an aged maid dressed in black appeared carrying a large tray of sandwiches—heaps of pita bread loaves sliced in half and stuffed with boiled meat. As soon as the front of the tray appeared through the opening of the door, the throng set upon these voraciously, causing the maid to thrust the whole thing at them, at which a fierce battle immediately broke out, the hands snatching at the meat sandwiches and the shouts swelling and quickly turning into screams and horrible insults. Kamil el-Zahhar stood on the dais watching the battling throng. He remained calm, not intervening with a single word, and eventually the battle came to an end and the throng dispersed—each with his booty—and little by little the room emptied completely. Then he stood up, closed the door, and sat down on the nearest chair.

◈

What had upset Mr. el-Zahhar? The celebration had been wonderful and his speech on Mustafa el-Nahhas extremely well received. He had been able to refute all the scurrilous lies Abdel Nasser had put into people's heads. He had told them how el-Nahhas Pasha had stood like a lion against the British and the high-handed king and demonstrated with cogent arguments that the February 4 Incident ought to be held to Mustafa el-Nahhas's credit and not against him.* His eloquence had convinced everyone present and their hands and throats had burned from all the clapping and shouting. Everything was as it should be, so what was it that was upsetting him? The truth is that Kamil el-Zahhar was one of those excessively sensitive people whom the merest word can gladden or wound to the utmost degree, and this evening the sight of the public fighting over the meat had shocked him. He was well aware that they were poor and he knew the faces of many of them but that the struggle over the food should have reached such an appalling level! And who were

---

* On February 4, 1942, British troops surrounded the royal palace in Cairo and forced King Farouk to accept a Wafd Party government led by Mustafa el-Nahhas.

the people involved? The very ones who had applauded and sometimes cheered for the Wafd and its leader! This thought gave Mr. el-Zahhar pause when he considered their devotion to the principles of the Wafd, and here his wife Dawlat's words as she handed him the five hundred pounds that he was to spend on the celebration returned to bother him. She had told him, with an affectionate smile, "Take this, Kamil, and may the Lord support you in your good works. Even if those people do just come to eat at our expense, it's the intention that God rewards."

The sharp intractable idea that kept sawing at his brain was that the Wafd was dead. Abdel Nasser had failed at everything else but he'd succeeded in cutting the Egyptians off from their past, and a generation had thus grown up that didn't know, and didn't want to know, anything about the Wafd and its leaders. How did Mr. el-Zahhar's children, Mustafa and Zeinab, look at him when he talked to them of Mustafa el-Nahhas? With a polite smile and an indifferent eye, and were it not for their respect for him they would openly make fun of him and his leader. It was not their fault, it was what they'd been taught in Abdel Nasser's schools. "What's happened to the world?" muttered Mr. el-Zahhar as he stretched his legs out and sank back into the chair, contemplating the picture of el-Nahhas on the wall. The Leader was wearing court dress and his chest was adorned with glittering stars; draped over his shoulder was the red sash of the judiciary, a silver sword dangled from his hip, and on his kindly face was a beautiful smile, full of nobility and patriotism.

Mr. el-Zahhar closed his eyes and images from the distant past welled up from within his memory. He saw himself as a student at Sa'idiya Secondary borne on the others' shoulders in a crowded demonstration and shouting out the slogans, the other students taking up the cry: "Long Live Egypt—Independent and Free!" The demonstration crosses University Avenue and in no time the students from the Faculty of Engineering have joined them. Enthusiasm reaches fever pitch and the slogans roar out, piercing the skies. The British try to disperse them but in vain. Then they open fire, the bullets whine, and the martyrs fall, crying aloud the name of Egypt. On the evening, he rushes to el-Nahhas's villa in Garden City, where he sees the great men of the nation standing in the hallway and waiting. But he . . . he, Kamil el-Zahhar, leader of the Sa'idiya students, who is not yet twenty years old, he is let in straight away and the Leader welcomes him and when el-Zahhar bends over to kiss his hand, el-Nahhas pulls it away with expressions of pious disavowal and says, "Zahhar, you are my son. A son of the Wafd. In you I see my own youth."

How happy he had been that day! Where had it all gone? How strange life was! One day he said proudly to his companions at the Sa'idiya, "I shall be prime minister of Egypt. I'm sure of it." He almost laughed at himself in derision. And the years had quickly passed and he had retired as a Department of Social Insurance employee like thousands of ordinary people. People had forgotten him just as they had forgotten Mustafa el-Nahhas.

Mr. el-Zahhar was tired and sad. Suddenly, however, he was overcome by a sense of ease. A mysterious and comforting sensation filled him and immediately afterward a strong light dazzled him, a light that shone and burned and moved closer until he felt something like a sharp slap across his face. Mr. el-Zahhar leaped up in terror and ran and looked out of the room, but when he saw the picture on the wall, astonishment rooted him to the spot: the picture was moving. The Leader's smile broadened, then he moved his right arm, and in a second he had descended from the picture. Himself. The Leader Mustafa el-Nahhas, in his brocaded frock coat studded with decorations and his tarboosh, standing before him and smiling. El-Zahhar started toward him, bent over his hand to kiss it, and embraced him, crying out, "Master! Where have you been?"

"I was dead, Zahhar. Then I prayed God would resurrect me and He answered my prayer."

El-Zahhar stared at the Leader.

"I see you are astonished at my return, Zahhar. He says in His Holy Book, *'Say, Who shall quicken the bones when they are decayed? Say, He shall quicken them who originated them the first time.'"*

"The Almighty has spoken truly, Master," muttered el-Zahhar. Then he continued in a trembling voice, "Most Lofty Excellency, save the Egypt for which you gave your life!"

The Leader shook his head and mumbled sorrowfully, "I know, Zahhar. In the Other World, I follow events day by day."

"What is to be done, Master? How are we to extricate Egypt from its predicament?"

"The motto of the Wafd is unchanging, Zahhar. 'Constitution and democracy.'"

"But the people have changed, O Leader of the Valley of the Nile. No one cares any more about the constitution. All people care about is filling their bellies."

"They are not to be blamed, Zahhar. Prices are high, many are poor, and life is hard. But a better life can only come through democracy."

"No one understands that, Master. No one remembers the Wafd and el-Nahhas any longer."

The smile disappeared from the Leader's face, his eyes clouded over, and he said earnestly, "Do not despair, Zahhar. Egypt will never die. It is 'God's Quiver on Earth.' A new generation of youth will emerge who know the worth of the Wafd. Listen. A long and exhausting struggle lies ahead of us. Kamil, are you still true to the Covenant?"

"My life is Egypt's and its Leader's!" exclaimed Mr el-Zahhar, with passion.

"Excellent. Let us start right away. I shall give you one day. I want you to gather your comrades and wait for me on Monday, at eight in the morning. Peace be upon you."

The Leader's face started to grow dim, his regard changed and he seemed to be looking at something far away on the horizon. In a strained voice he said, as he retreated backward toward the wall, "I have to go back up. I have an appointment now in Heaven. I wish you good fortune."

El-Zahhar rushed after him, asking urgently, "Where shall we wait for you, Master?"

"Before the House of the Nation."*

The Leader uttered these words with difficulty, having now become fully stuck to the wall. El-Zahhar stretched out his hand to grasp hold of him but he was seized by a sudden

---

* *The House of the Nation, the symbolic home of the Wafd Party, was the house of the nationalist leader and founder of the party, Saad Zaghloul (1859–1927). It is now a museum.*

violent dizziness and when he came to, the picture of Mustafa el-Nahhas had returned to its original state.

◈

Muhammad Bey Bassiouni's morning routine never varied. He would wake up, bathe, and change out of his pajamas. Then he would take a stroll in his *robe de chambre* in the garden of the villa in el-Maadi. Borai would have brought the newspapers and he would sit and read them in the garden, using his magnifying glass, while he sipped his cup of warm milk. Over the last few years, Bassiouni Bey had been subjected to numerous health crises and these had had their impact on his powers of concentration. It followed that that morning, when confronted with the sight of Kamil el-Zahhar standing in front of him, he was briefly confused. Then he welcomed him and no sooner had Mr. el-Zahhar sat down than he began telling him that the Leader, Mustafa el-Nahhas, had visited him the night before, at which point Bassiouni looked hard at him from behind his glasses and said to him, "Who did you say visited you yesterday, Kamil Bey?"

"El-Nahhas Pasha. He came out of the picture in the sitting room," responded el-Zahhar.

"Ah!" muttered Bassiouni Bey, who then continued to listen to el-Zahhar with a polite smile and no interest. El-Zahhar immediately fixed his eyes on him reproachfully, saying, "Don't you believe me, Bassiouni Bey?"

"Please, Kamil Bey. Of course I believe you," Bassiouni replied politely, the smile never leaving his lips.

The old man doesn't believe me, and is making fun of me, thought el-Zahhar, furious as he emerged from the door of the villa, and when he had seated himself in the taxi, he said, "I am not mad. I have never in my life been saner than I am today. Mustafa el-Nahhas touched my hand and spoke to me. That is a certain truth, and tomorrow el-Nahhas Pasha will come back to me. I will take him with me everywhere. We will go together to the press, to the Lower House, and we will request a meeting with the President of the Republic himself. We—the Leader and I—will be headlines in Tuesday's newspapers and then we shall see what Muhammad Bassiouni says."

The taxi stopped in front of the house of Sheikh Ali Sahhab on Murad Street just as Sheikh Ali completed the midmorning prayer, and the sheikh sat down, passing his prayer beads through his fingers, and welcomed his friend Kamil el-Zahhar. The latter wasted no time in recounting to him what had happened, in detail. Silence reigned for a moment, and then Sheikh Ali rumbled in his deep voice, "A strange story indeed!"

At which el-Zahhar cried out, "Listen, Sheikh Ali! If you don't believe me, tell me and I'll go."

Sheikh Ali answered, soothingly, "Of course I believe you, Kamil. We've known each other all our lives. And spirits do exist: *They will question thee concerning the Spirit. Say, 'The Spirit is of the bidding of my Lord'* (the Almighty has spoken truly). Only . . . are you sure it was el-Nahhas Pasha?"

El-Zahhar jumped up, for emphasis, and said, "I saw el-Nahhas Pasha as clearly as I see you now, and he spoke to me. Listen. Tomorrow I'm going to meet His Excellency the Pasha. Will you come with me or not?"

Deep thought appeared on the sheikh's face, and after a second he stood up, took el-Zahhar's hand to shake it, and said, "I'll come with you."

❖

Could Mr. el-Zahhar sleep that night? He lay next to his wife, Dawlat, in the dark and started smoking and thinking about the coming day. Of course, it would be a surprise for everyone, but what after? He would organize with the Leader vast campaigns. They would tour the whole of Egypt. Every Egyptian must see the Leader and hear him, in the cities, in the hamlets, and in the Bedouin encampments. And at the first elections the Wafd would sweep the field, as usual, and Mustafa el-Nahhas would form a Wafdist cabinet, in which el-Zahhar would be a minister. He would choose either the Treasury or the Economy. That was his field. Foreign Affairs was sensitive and dangerous and the Interior was not his type of thing at all. Dawlat woke up, turned on the light, and looked at him anxiously.

"Why aren't you asleep, Kamil?"

"It's nothing."

If the partner of his life only knew what tomorrow held! *My darling Dawlat, in less than a year you will be the minister's wife. Didn't you put up with Kamil el-Zahhar the insurance department employee for a quarter of a century without grumbling or complaining? Pluck then, my high-born rose, the fruits of your long and patient wait! You will make the pilgrimage to God's Holy House as you have always wanted, and then it'll be summers in Europe for you, me, and my dear Mustafa and Zeinab.* El-Zahhar drew close to his wife, planted a kiss on her brow, and whispered tenderly, "Goodnight" and pretended to sleep. At precisely seven o'clock the next morning, he leaped out of bed and a quarter of an hour later was running down the empty street making for the House of the Nation. He had to arrive before the Leader. He might wait for the Leader, but certainly not the other way round!

The House of the Nation was closed and on the door there was a brass plate announcing "House of the Nation Museum. Open 10–3 except Fridays."

The building was old and covered with thick layers of dust, the garden neglected and bleak. El-Zahhar felt sad and determined privately that the first task of the new cabinet would be to restore the House of the Nation. It was now a quarter to eight. Sheikh Ali Sahhab had arrived a minute ago, shaken el-Zahhar's hand, and stood next to him on the sidewalk. Then a black Cadillac appeared gliding along at the end of the street. It drew closer until it stopped in front of the two friends and Muhammad Bey Bassiouni got out. When el-Zahhar rushed over to him, Bassiouni shook his hand and got the first word in by saying excitedly, "El-Nahhas will come, Kamil. El-Nahhas never breaks an appointment."

It was exactly eight o'clock. The street was crowded with cars and pedestrians, on the sidewalk opposite people had gathered around a stall selling bean sandwiches, everywhere troops of employees from the nearby ministry buildings were running to get to work on time, and in front of the House of the Nation the three—Mr. Kamil el-Zahhar, Sheikh Ali Sahhab, and Muhammad Bey Bassiouni—continued to stand, gazing eagerly toward the end of the street where, in a few moments, the August Leader, His Most Lofty Excellency Mustafa el-Nahhas Pasha would arrive.

A Look into Nagi's Face

MY SCHOOL. The old building with its windows, rounded balconies, and huge pillars appears in the early morning mist like an abandoned castle. The wooden gate opens slowly to reveal the spacious courtyard with its huge bare trees whose dry yellow leaves are spread over the ground and we crush them underfoot as we play in the playground so that they make a soft crackling sound and break into little pieces. We are sitting in the classroom in our blue smocks, sewn with the venerable school's motto, listening to the Frère, our teacher. I remember his aged face and bald patch, his glasses, blue eyes, dull-colored military boots and billowing white robe. On his chest was the imposing image of a cross and in his hand his cane. Ah, that long thin cane, painful as a razorblade, quick as a bullet.

The Frère roams among us, reading from the book, his voice monotonous, endlessly repeating itself. The air in the classroom is still, impending sleepiness teases me, and through the window next to me I look out onto the cars, the passersby, and Uncle Kamil, who sells doum fruit. I entertain myself by watching the street until I am brought to my senses by the sting of the cane on my back and the Frère's voice breaking in on my thoughts. "Continue reading!"

I die. I stare trembling at the book but the small lines run into one another in front of my eyes.

"Put your hand out!"

The Frère is in front of me brandishing his cane in the air. There is no way out. I extend my hand and he grips it and brings the cane down on it. I scream and cry and beg him to forgive me, but he strikes and strikes and then lets me fall back onto my seat. I look tearfully at the boys around me. I call on them to be my witnesses, but they pretend to be reading and following the lesson; they ignore me, and, if I were to appeal to them now, they would answer as one, feigning innocence, "What happened to you? We didn't see anything and we don't know anything." In fact, after this incident, as soon as the Frère asks a question, they leap up from their seats and thrust their hands into the air, as though, through their eagerness to answer, they are annihilating any connection to me; as though they are saying to the Frère, "He's the one who disobeyed you. We, however, are your ever faithful students."

My hand hurt and I was crying loudly but the Frère paid no attention. He resumed reading as though nothing had happened, except that maybe his thin lips mumbled a little, as if saying, threateningly, "Observe! This is the reward of him who disobeys." And who would dare? We have submitted to you, O Teacher, and obeyed your orders and become—under the influence of time and obedience—parts of you, like your finger: you crook us and bend us and do with us as you will. Sometimes the Frère is happy, and he smiles and jokingly calls us by the names of various animals. Immediately, we catch the signal, bursting into raucous laughter and shouting at the tops of our voices and stamping our feet, and then it's as though we are letting out all at one go everything we have long hidden beneath the surface of our polite, still faces. Things come to an end just as they began, with a gesture or a light cough from the Frère, or a look that takes us unawares and stops us in our tracks. Then we shrink; there's not a voice or a breath to be heard as we know well that the slightest suggestion of indiscipline now means certain perdition, the very thought of which terrifies us as much as any mythical monster of the dark.

❖

Then Nagi came. That morning he stood at the door to the classroom, regarding us with his startled, honey-colored eyes. He dazzled us, he was so beautiful. His face was white and pale, his chestnut hair smooth and flowing, his smock neat and well ironed, his leather bag—unlike our bulging versions—high-quality and gleaming, without patch or sign of wear. Even his sandwiches were delicate and white, like him—slices of snow-white, foreign-style bread, spread with butter, which he carried in a smart transparent bag like the halvah that we ate on our birthdays. The Frère said, "This is your new classmate, Nagi." Then he looked around searching for a place for him, and the place next to mine was vacant, and I wished. . . . Is it enough for us to wish hard for something to come true? The Frère was pointing to where I was sitting and Nagi was approaching me, whispering a greeting, and sitting down, and I could smell the faint aroma that emanated from his clothes. I would spend the rest of that day examining him and sniffing him until the bell rang and we could talk. He told me that his mother was French and his father Egyptian and I told him about myself. I waited with him at the door to the school until his luxurious car arrived, the driver descending and picking up his bag, and I asked him urgently as I shook his hand, "Are we friends, Nagi?" and he nodded and got in. At home in the kitchen, I tugged at my mother's dress so hard that the hot food almost spilled all over her. I wanted her to listen while I told her about Nagi. From then on I controlled myself and would imitate his face, drawing in my features in front of the mirror in the hope of seeing the two dimples that appeared on Nagi's when he smiled.

In no time, Nagi settled into his place at the pinnacle of the class. He was the most beautiful one among us and the cleverest. A flash from his eyes meant an hour of explanation by the Frère, and we would follow along with the two of them, panting and struggling to keep up, and in the end we would stare at the blackboard and nod our heads as though we understood. Even our French accents seemed heavy beside Nagi's fluent, refined speech, his French being like the Frère's, or perhaps better. Then we discovered, little by little, that Nagi wasn't afraid like us. His face didn't blanch, his voice didn't shake, and his eyes didn't seek refuge in the ceiling or the floor. He would stand in front of the Frère, pull himself up to his full height, and speak to him with a clarity and confidence that increased each time; and each time we expected the accident to happen, as though Nagi were a speeding car rushing headlong toward the top of a mountain behind which lay a sheer cliff. We would shut our eyes and wait for the sound of the terrible crash, but it didn't happen. On the contrary, the Frère humored Nagi and was patient with him, and we were delighted. We never asked ourselves, "Why does the Frère prefer Nagi to us?"

We never asked because we loved Nagi and when we loved someone it was as though they were us, as though it were us that were standing tall before the Frère. We were all Nagi. We weren't afraid and we weren't beaten (even though in fact we were beaten, daily) and we would crowd around him in the playground, begging him to play with us and competing at explaining the game to him—and how proud the one who made him smile! Nagi was happy and we were happy with him, until that day.

The Frère was collecting the assignment books as usual and Nagi stood up in front of him and said in his confident voice, "I'm sorry, I forgot mine at home." The Frère's face twitched. Then he moved his lips as though making his mind up about something and said, "Put your hand out!"

But Nagi didn't put his hand out and didn't budge and the Frère's voice rose terrifyingly as he shouted, "Put your hand out!"

Nagi remains as unmoving as a rock, and we rush up to him to support him from behind with our little trembling hands, but the Frère is bellowing and raises his hand high in the air and brings it down on Nagi's face, at which we all scream, but we don't make any noise and it's clear that everything we think we've done didn't happen because Nagi's face reddens and he shouts, "Hitting is not allowed!"—at which the Frère's voice roars out like thunder as he cries, "Out, you wretch! I'll show you how to behave!"

Short, hurried, shaky footsteps are followed by long, resolute, merciless footsteps, and as soon as they have left classroom we go crazy, jumping up from our places and running and screaming a hundred times, as though to make the Frère hear, "Hitting is *not allowed*!" while a multitude of scenarios jostle before our eyes, all of which end with the Frère lying on the ground, the blood running from his face and Nagi next to him, his chest swollen with pride and his hands on hips, like the triumphant hero of an adventure movie.

The Frère returned alone and set about collecting the books again, but in vain. What had happened had happened and something had changed and student after student turned out to have forgotten his assignment book, but the Frère didn't strike any of them; he made an angry gesture with his hand, averted his face, and then moved on as though he could have struck the boy but was fed up with everything. But you were lying, Teacher; you had been broken, and we saw you then with new eyes and we found you to be ordinary, and if we'd stripped you of your friar's robe, you would have been just like anybody else on the street.

The day passed and anxiety over Nagi gnawed at us. At home in the evening, we told what had happened. Our mothers didn't give us their full attention and our fathers were disturbed by the idea of rebellion so they sought to divert us. Next morning, Nagi was back. He stood with us in the lineup and we crowded round him with a thousand questions, but he didn't answer, he just smiled and kept silent. His face was neither pale nor miserable. Nor was it, however, his face of yesterday. The period started, Nagi sat down, and the Frère started explaining the lesson as usual. After a little while, as though by agreement, the Frère called Nagi from his place and the two of them stood facing us. In threatening tones, the Frère said, "I'm going to the principal's office for a few minutes and Nagi will be in charge. Anyone whose name Nagi writes down gets ten strokes of the cane!"

Nagi stands over us, his hands clasped behind his back, his eyes widening as he scans us slowly, searching for any infraction. All the boys play it safe, arms folded in front of them and heads lowered in submission as they read, and they dart warning glances at me, as if to say, "Everything's changed. Play it safe," but I don't play it safe. Why would I need to be safe from Nagi when I'm his friend?

I suddenly find myself calling out, "Nagi!" as though I were trying to keep him with me, to cling on to him. But he pushes me violently away and then turns to the blackboard and writes my name, and the Frère comes and he gives me ten strokes with the cane in front of the class.

Here I am. Tears wet my face, my hand stings, and I turn to Nagi, who stands forever next to the Frère. I keep looking at him. Maybe he will cover his gaze just once.

Why, Sayed?
(A Question)

WHY, MY DEAR, GOOD SAYED ABD EL-TAWWAB? It wasn't the first time, and what happened was no surprise to you. Not to mention that the young man was polite and pleasant and you were the one who made a play for him. When you saw him get off the bus in front of the museum, his camera over his shoulder, his quiet demeanor appealed to you. He wasn't trying to attract attention like the others. You, Sayed, were the one who approached him and started a conversation by saying hello and telling him you were an Egyptian boy who would like to make his acquaintance. His blue eyes widened in surprise. Then his lips parted in a welcoming smile that was not without a certain suspicion, which you quickly dispelled with your warm, fluent speech. Weren't you happy with him in the restaurant? You had a long, sentimental talk, and he invited you to have a drink with him after dinner and like an old friend opened his heart to you, telling you that he worked in a hospital in Boston, while you told him about your diploma in commerce. When you calculated your salary for him in dollars, he couldn't believe it at first and when you had convinced him, he laughed so long you couldn't help yourself and you laughed too.

If it's what the elevator operator at the hotel said to you, he is, when it comes down to it, nothing but a servant, and what do you, Sayed, care what servants say about you? And anyway, what happened in the room? The young man told you how attached he was to his mother and showed you her photo and when you told him she looked like your aunt, he said to you, laughing, that you must really be relatives then. He was slightly drunk but the alcohol only made him more agreeable. And when you asked him, Sayed, did he hesitate? Did he not hasten to stuff the hundred-dollar bill into your pocket? And after it was over—and, as you know well, Sayed, it isn't always so—he wasn't rude and insensitive, he remained tactful with you to the end. You have his address in Boston on you now and, who knows, maybe you'll visit him there one day. And here you are now, Sayed, sitting and having breakfast at the Meridien, eating and drinking like a king, and all you have to do is to put the check on Room No. 511 and in half an hour the banks will be open and you'll go to the nearest one, to any bank that will change the hundred dollars while you wait. So what's the problem? Why, Sayed, are you all of a sudden crying now, like a child?

Games

ALL OF US IN FIFTH ELEMENTARY used to look forward to gym class with total impatience. On Tuesday mornings, we'd remove our school uniforms and put on our gym clothes—"white shorts, white undershirt, and tennis shoes." Miss Souad, the gym teacher, would gather us in the playground and we'd stand in three parallel lines and do exercises for a quarter of an hour. Then we'd play ball for the rest of the period.

Our schoolmate Muhammad el-Dawakhli did not join us for gym because he was extremely fat. With his huge body, his flabby belly, and his large buttocks, he couldn't get into the shorts like us or lie on his back and raise his legs in the air as we did in exercises. He couldn't even play ball with us—he sweated too much and ran out of breath at the slightest effort. From this an essentially unspoken agreement developed by which Miss Souad ignored el-Dawakhli completely and he spent the gym period sitting on the steps that led up to the classrooms. There he would sit, wearing his school clothes of navy jacket and long gray pants, observing us in silence. We, on the other hand, no sooner had Miss Souad thrown us the inflatable ball with its black and white squares, would as one let out a loud cry of "Heeeeeey!" snatch up the ball, and plunge into a fierce discussion which would last until we had reached a suitable division into two teams. The shared goal would be marked out with two bricks and as soon as play started we would forget everything, running with the ball, dodging, scoring goals, and imitating the famous players we saw on television: the moment one of us scored a goal, his teammates would rush up to him and kiss him and congratulate him, while he'd fall to the ground and thank God for the goal or run off raising his hands toward the trees that lined either side of the playground, pretending that they were the stands, crammed with the roaring crowd.

At such moments, we would forget el-Dawakhli completely. We would think of him only if there was a dispute over some play, when we would turn to him in his distant seat and cry excitedly, "Was that a goal, Dawakhli?"

When this happened, el-Dawakhli would stand up, his plump face taking on a serious mien, hurry over to us, stretch out his arm in the direction of the play, and say, panting, "The ball came from here. So it's a goal, a hundred percent."

Having thus delivered himself of his conclusive decision and performed his duty, he'd return to the stands, sit down, and continue watching.

Now, when I think back, I realize how much el-Dawakhli must have longed to play with us and how much he must have wished he had a small, ordinary body like ours, instead of his comically fat one. But we were young, too young to understand. We thought of him as a huge, odd creature made to incite laughter and entertain, just like the elephants and bears that we went to the circus to see. Indeed, as far as we were concerned, making fun of el-Dawakhli was a temptation we could never resist. We were always insulting him for being so obese, to the extent even that some of the boys became veritable experts at getting a rise out of him. One might, for example, get up from his desk in the minutes between one class and the next with a stupid, quarrelsome expression on his face, rush over to where el-Dawakhli was sitting, and pounce on him—just like that, for no reason and without saying a word—giving him a hard slap on the back of his neck, and then running; or snatch a copy book or a pen from him; or—and this was the very least that duty demanded—stand at a safe distance in front of him and start making fun of him in a loud voice, saying, for example, "Hey, Dawakhli you bullock, what makes you so fat? What do they feed you at home, you mule, you pig?" and keep it up until the rest of the boys were howling with laughter

And el-Dawakhli would submit to these attacks, aware that he was powerless to catch his assailant if he chased him and knowing from experience that resistance only increased their fury. He would, therefore, remain seated, saying nothing, his body stuffed behind the desk, pretending that he hadn't heard, or sometimes with an abject, pale, wan smile on his face that pleaded with his assailant to desist. When one of them slapped him and ran, el-Dawakhli would turn toward us, the ones who were laughing, his face still clouded with the effect of the blow, and then sigh and shake his head as though to ask us in amazement, "What's wrong with that boy?"

Despite all of which, el-Dawakhli made every effort to ingratiate himself with us. He'd willingly lend us anything as soon as we asked for it. He'd give us a sandwich or an exercise book or even a pen during an exam, should one of us have forgotten his, and on his own initiative he'd phone any student who was absent and dictate what he'd missed to him. The moment that el-Dawakhli saw you in the playground, he'd start talking to you about something that you were interested in—the increase in the school fees, or how difficult geography was—as though to distract your attention from his person, or he'd take you by the hand and pull you aside and bend over and whisper in the accents of one imparting an important secret that he'd heard that the Arabic teacher was going to call a pop quiz tomorrow, so you'd better get ready; then he'd pat you affectionately on the shoulder and move away.

El-Dawakhli did this so that we'd like him, or, at the least, so that his niceness to us would shame us into not hurting him any more, but all his efforts were in vain. We'd listen to his exciting news, accept his help, and thank him, but our exchanges with him remained tense and surrounded by danger, coming at a certain point to teeter on the edge of embarrassment and then suddenly flipping us back into our mockery and insults.

Miss Souad disappeared and we heard that she'd been transferred to another school. In her place they brought Mr. Hamid, who was extremely tall, with piercing wide eyes and a frowning face, and whose long thin cane with the pointed end that stung our backs and our hands if we slacked off a little during the exercises never left his hand. He was a new teacher, and severe, and, as soon as he saw el-Dawakhli sitting on the steps in his school uniform, he called him over and asked him why he wasn't wearing his gym clothes. El-Dawakhli hung his head and didn't answer, and the teacher warned him that he'd better turn up in his uniform the next time.

In the playground, we surrounded el-Dawakhli and asked him about it and he told us very plainly that he'd never wear gym clothes. He asserted that students who had special 'circumstances' such as his own were forbidden to wear gym clothes, and everyone knew that.

Despite el-Dawakhli's assertion, something about his voice and his eyes made us feel that he was in a tight spot and didn't know what to do. The next time we had gym, we took our places in the lines in readiness for the exercises. We looked around for el-Dawakhli but couldn't find him, and he wasn't sitting on the steps as he usually did. Our eyes scanned the whole playground until we discovered him: he was there, hiding behind the large tree next to the cafeteria. He had concealed his body behind the huge trunk, his head peering round it to watch what was going on, very like an ostrich trying to disappear. But in vain: the teacher spotted him and yelled out his name, so el-Dawakhli hurried over to him. The teacher forestalled him by saying in a threatening voice, "Did you bring your gym clothes?"

El-Dawakhli was silent for a moment. Then, to our astonishment, he nodded his head, and the teacher said, "Go and get changed and come back here."

A murmur ran through the boys. This was the bombshell of the season. El-Dawakhli wearing shorts and gym clothes?

We were going to die of laughter at the sight and lay into him with mockery and teasing until he could take no more. We were possessed by an overweening curiosity and a powerful, malign desire of the sort that takes over the people watching a wrestling match. We wanted at that moment to harm and hurt and enjoy. Our eyes hung on the steps, on which, after a moment, el-Dawakhli would reappear. We were restless with eagerness, like young wild animals smacking their lips in anticipation of the prey. We didn't have to wait long. There was el-Dawakhli coming down the stairs looking much stranger than we'd even imagined. The gym shirt made his breasts stick out like a woman's and his big belly hung down and shook this way and that. The shining whiteness of his fat thighs, and his incredible buttocks, divided by the shorts into two closely spaced segments of equal size, one rising while the other fell, were there for all to see.

A gale of laughter rang out. All of us were consumed with hilarity—even the teacher, whose lips parted in a wide grin. We began clapping, whistling, and shouting, "El-Dawakhli!" El-Dawakhli had to cross the playground to get to us but we couldn't contain our impatience and rushed over to him and formed a circle around him, laughing and applauding. El-Dawakhli started behaving in a strange way. He started laughing and pretending that he couldn't stop himself. Then he started to walk doubled over so as to exaggerate the way his buttocks stuck out, and to pat his belly. He'd made up his mind to make himself as much of a laughingstock as he could and this was his way of getting out of the situation, as though telling us, "See? I'm so funny I make even myself laugh. What more do you want?"

This approach displeased us somewhat. El-Dawakhli's artificial laughter diluted the strength of our mockery. Without his pain and anger our joy was incomplete, and our wicked impulse drove us imperiously on to the end, as though we were possessed by demons; we didn't even pay attention to the teacher calling us from behind to come back. We went up to el-Dawakhli and set about assiduously abusing him, more than one falling on him and slapping him and pulling him. At that instant, we were no longer laughing at his appearance; we were now laughing simply to cause him pain, so that we could break that shell of indifference under which he hid his sorrow. And el-Dawakhli would not give in. He went on faking his laugh and walking doubled over, but we increased the attack further and further until one of us said something about him suckling babies with his breasts and we burst into even greater laughter. It was only at that point that el-Dawakhli stopped walking and started flinging his arms about violently in an attempt to hit us. All his blows went wide, however, and he fastened his eyes on us and opened his mouth to say something. Then his lips quivered and he burst into tears.

Boxer Puppies, All Colors

"FAWWAZ HUSSEIN" IS THE NAME he'll whisper to you, introducing himself, and when you see him you're sure to find him lovable, for Fawwaz Hussein is likeable. He is also a bit of a dandy, as witnessed by his Vaseline-slicked hair and his forelock, in the style of Anwar Wagdi, not to mention the broad leather belt that encircles his huge paunch and at whose midpoint is a brass buckle on which "LOVE" is written in English, and, finally, the shiny shoes with the pointed tips and wedge heels that Fawwaz favors above all other kinds. Though all these things went out of fashion twenty years ago, when Fawwaz was a young man, he still takes good care of them and will sometimes be overcome by a sense of how smart they are and you'll catch him contemplating in an admiring and self-satisfied way, as he talks to you, the buckle on his belt or the tips of his shoes. Fawwaz Hussein is also polite, so polite that he makes one feel embarrassed.

He veritably drips politeness. As soon as he sees you, he runs over to shake your hand, bowing so deeply before you that his back forms a bow, as though there's nothing he'd love more in the world than for his huge body to shrink and dwindle, out of respect for your honorable presence. When he talks to you, he whispers, lowers his eyes, and forms his thick lips into an "O," puckering them up till they look like the beak of a tiny, innocent bird. Why not then love Fawwaz?

Despite all that politeness and all that submissiveness, the answer is known to the residents of Sugar-and-Lime Alley, where Fawwaz is accustomed to sit, in the café at its top end. These residents have seen Fawwaz fight with switch blades and chairs, on which occasions he pushes his lips forward in preparation, fixes his opponent with a look of fire, and then initiates the battle with a roaring flood of insults most of which turn on the latter's mother's private life. They will never forget the day when Fawwaz got into a fight with Sergeant-Major Abd el-Ghani following a game of cards they'd been playing for money. Fawwaz gathered the children of the alley and went and stood with them outside Abd el-Ghani's house by the railroad tracks and started singing in his deep, cracked voice, the children gleefully repeating after him, "Mrs. Sergeant-Major, you great fat turd, you eat green beans and shit bean curd." Such is the Fawwaz Hussein known to the people of the alley, but they don't know everything. No one, for example, knows where Fawwaz works. Sometimes he has money, but more often he's broke.

On one particular morning, Fawwaz was sitting in the café as usual drinking tea with milk and smoking a water-pipe when a boy passed in front of him carrying a puppy on his shoulder. The boy was barefoot and wearing an old, torn gallabiya. The dog, on the other hand, had sleek black hair and looked beautiful, and there was a red collar with a bow round its neck.

"You boy, come here," cried Fawwaz, an idea flashing through his mind. The boy approached, looking fearfully at Fawwaz.

"Where did you get that dog?" Fawwaz asked him in threatening tones.

"From el-Maadi."

"You stole it. I'll give you hell," cried Fawwaz, before delivering a hard blow to the boy's face, causing him to throw the dog down and show Fawwaz his heels.

Fawwaz grabbed the dog and picked it up; it had a strange appearance, with a sagging belly, short legs, and a sloping face. Then he got it a small bone to chew from the kebab seller's and sat down and smoked his pipe and thought, "What can I do with this dog?"

The dog was from el-Maadi and had to be worth a lot; once he'd heard that boxers could fetch as much as a hundred pounds. After some thought and meditation, Fawwaz arrived at the solution, and two days later an advertisement appeared in *al-Ahram* stating, "Dogs for sale, pedigree Boxers, all colors available," followed by the telephone number of the café.

From morning on Fawwaz sat next to the telephone answering enquiries and giving out his address in Sugar-and-Lime Alley, and a little before noon the first "client" showed up when a large black Mercedes entered the alley and a white-haired man of imposing appearance wearing an overcoat of expensive black cloth descended. His face was as red as an Englishman's and for a moment Fawwaz thought he must be a foreigner. Fawwaz hurried over to the man and welcomed him with elaborate courtesy, bringing him a chair and ordering him a glass of tea with milk but not, naturally, inviting him to share the waterpipe. Then he turned to him and said—smiling, lowering his eyes, and extending his lips—"What can I do for you, sir?"

"I've come to see you about the dogs, actually, my dear sir."

Fawwaz relaxed at the sound of "my dear sir" and immediately rose and left, returning after a few minutes with the dog, which he had been keeping tied up next to the stand where they made the coffee, on his shoulder. The man looked the dog over carefully, before picking it up and playing with it while examining it with an expert hand. While this was going on, Fawwaz kept up a constant stream of words.

"This dog, sir, is the last one left. I've sold three and this is the fourth. Of course, Your Excellency is well aware that boxers are very hard to find these days. Lots of people are looking and they just can't find any." Then, with an unexpected movement, Fawwaz extended his hand and took hold of the gentleman's, saying, "Honest to God, my dear friend, I have a very good feeling about you and everything tells me this boxer should be yours, so what do you say?"

"It's very good of you. But this dog isn't a boxer."

"What?" cried Fawwaz, as though to deny what the man had said and looking around him as if seeking someone who would see justice done in the face of this false accusation.

"What a thing to say, sir! That dog's a boxer through and through. Take a good look and you'll see. Look! He's telling you, 'I'm a boxer.' Is that any way to talk?"

The gentleman's smile widened. He was quite sure of himself.

"My dear fellow, boxers are utterly different. I've been a dog lover for forty years."

"What kind is it, then?" mumbled Fawwaz, finally submitting and inwardly cursing customer and dog alike, while the twenty pounds he'd paid for the advertisement loomed up to torture him.

"Pekinese."

"So what? It doesn't matter. The point is, how much will you pay for it?"

Fawwaz said this wearily, having decided to get rid of the miserable dog at any price.

The gentleman was silent for a moment as he affectionately contemplated the dog, and the dog, as though somehow aware of what was going on, jumped up at the man, extending his nose and licking his face.

"I'll pay three hundred."

It took Fawwaz a moment to absorb the shock. Then he said in loud tones, "Hold on, that's just not right! Shame upon Your Excellency! A . . . (but he just couldn't get his tongue round the wretched name) . . . a pedigree dog like that and you tell me three hundred pounds? I mean, you ought to offer seven hundred, or six."

After some chaffering, the gentleman took three hundred and fifty pounds out of his pocket. Fawwaz counted them quickly and put them into the pocket of his pants. The gentleman put the dog on his shoulder, his face flushed with happiness, and Fawwaz escorted him to his car, then bowed and shook his hand in farewell.

After that he vanished and no more news was heard of Fawwaz Hussein in the café or the alley. No one knew why he had disappeared until word went round a little while ago that some young men from the alley had seen him early one morning prowling the streets of el-Maadi, hovering around outside the gardens there, and, as soon as he spotted a dog, throwing him a little bone from a bag he was carrying, then puckering up his lips and calling in a low voice, "Good doggy. Come here, doggy."

Mme Zitta Mendès,
A Last Image

1961

ON SUNDAYS MY FATHER WOULD TAKE ME with him to her house. The building, which was immensely tall, was situated halfway down Adly Street. The moment we went through the main door a waft of cool air would meet us. The lobby was of marble and spacious, the columns huge and round, and the giant Nubian doorkeeper would hurry ahead of us to call the elevator, retiring, after my father had pressed a banknote into his hand, with fervent thanks. From that point on, my father would wear a different face from the one I knew at home. At Tante Zitta's house, my father became gentle, courteous, playful, soft-spoken, tender, afire with emotion.

Written in French on the small brass plaque at the door of the apartment were the words "Mme Zitta Mendès," and she would open the door to us herself, looking radiant with her limpid, fresh, white face, her petite nose, her full lips made up with crimson lipstick, her blue, wide, and seemingly astonished eyes with their long, curling lashes, her smooth black hair that flowed over her shoulders, and the décolleté dress that revealed her ample chest and plump, creamy arms. Even her finger and toe nails were clean, elegant, carefully outlined, and painted in shiny red.

I shall long retain in my memory the image of Zitta as she opened the door—the image of the 'other woman' enhanced by the aroma of sin, the svelte mistress who draws you into her secret, velvety world tinged with pleasure and temptation. Tante Zitta would receive me with warm kisses and hugs, saying over and over again in French, "Welcome, young man!" while behind her would appear Antoine, her son, who was two years older than I—a slim, tall youth whose black hair covered the upper part of his brow and the freckles on whose face made him look like the boy in the French reading book we used at school.

Antoine rarely spoke or smiled. He would observe us— me and my father—with an anxious look and purse his lips, then make a sudden move, standing or going to his room. He always seemed to have something important on his mind that he was on the verge of declaring but which he'd shy away from at the last minute. Even when I was playing with him in his room, he would apply himself to the game in silence, as though performing a duty. (Just once, he stopped in the middle of the game and asked me all of a sudden, "What does your father do?" I said, "He's a lawyer" and he responded quickly, "My father's a big doctor in America and when I'm older I'm going to go there." When I asked him disbelievingly, "And leave your mom?" he gave me an odd look and said nothing.) Antoine's disconcerting, difficult nature made my father and me treat him with caution.

So there we would sit, all together in the parlor. My father and Tante Zitta would be trying to hold an intense conversation and Antoine would be his usual aloof self, but I'd be giving it all I had: I'd flirt with Tante Zitta and surrender to her kisses, her strong, titillating perfume, and the feel of her warm, smooth skin. I'd tell her about my school and make up fabulous heroic deeds that I'd performed with my fellow students and she'd pretend that she believed me and make a show of astonishment and fear that I might get hurt in the course of one of these amazing 'feats.'

I was very fond of Tante Zitta and colluded totally with my father when each time on the way back he'd impress on me that I shouldn't tell my mother. I'd nod my head like a real man who could be relied on and when my mother, with her apprehensive, reluctant, alarming eyes, would ask me, I'd say, "Father and I went to the cinema," lying without either fear or the slightest sense of guilt or betrayal.

Zitta's magic world captivated me. I keep it in my heart. Even her apartment I can summon up in detail now as a model of ancient European elegance—the large mirror in the entrance and the curly wooden stand on which we would hang our coats, the round polished brass pots decorated with a lion's head on either side for the plants, the heavy, drawn drapes through which the subdued daylight filtered, the light-colored patterned wallpaper and set of dark brown armchairs with olive-green slip covers, and, in the corner, the large black piano (Zitta worked as a dancer at a nightclub on Elfi Street, which is where, I suppose, my father must have met her).

Tante Zitta would go into the kitchen to get the food ready and my father would draw Antoine and me close and put his hands on us and talk to us like an affectionate father chatting with his sons during a moment of rest. From time to time he would shout out in mock complaint about how long the food was taking and Zitta would answer laughingly from the kitchen. (I now take these touches of domesticity as evidence that my father was thinking of marrying her).

The luncheon table was a work of art—the shining white table cloth, the napkins ironed and folded with offhand elegance, the polished white plates with the knives, forks, and spoons laid round them in the same order. There would be a vase of roses, a jug of water, sparkling glasses, and a tall bottle lying on its side in a metal vessel filled with ice cubes. Tante Zitta's food was delicious and resembled that at the luxurious restaurants to which my father would occasionally take my mother and me. I would eat carefully and pretend to be full quickly, the way they'd taught me at home, so that no one might criticize me, but my father and Tante Zitta would be oblivious to everything, sitting next to one another, eating, drinking, whispering, and constantly laughing. Then my father would urge her to sing. At first she would refuse. Then she'd give in and sit down at the piano. Gradually the smile would disappear and her face would take on a serious expression as she ran her fingers over the keys and scattered, halting tunes rose from the keyboard. At a certain point, Zitta would bow her head and close her eyes as though trying to capture a particular idea. Then she would start to play. She would sing the songs of Edith Piaf—*Non, je ne regrette rien* and *La vie en rose*.

She had a melodious voice with a melancholy huskiness to it and when she got to the end she would remain for a few moments with her head bowed and her eyes closed, pressing on the keys with her fingers. I would clap enthusiastically and Antoine would remain silent, but my father's excitement would know no bounds. By this time he would have taken off his jacket and loosened his tie, and he would clap and shout, "Bravo!", hurrying to her side and planting a kiss on her forehead, or taking her hands in his and kissing them. Experience had taught us that this was a signal for me and Antoine to leave. Antoine would get up first, saying as he moved toward the door of the apartment, "Mama, we'll go outside and play." I can see now—with understanding and a smile—the face of my father, flushed with drink, alight with desire, as he searched impatiently through his pockets, then presented me and Antoine with two whole pounds, saying, as he waved us toward the door, "Tell you what. How about some ice-cream at New Kursaal after you've finished playing?"

◈

1996

The foreigners' table at Groppi's. All of them are old—Armenians and Greeks who have spent their lives in Egypt and kept going until they are completely alone. Their weekly date is at seven on Sunday mornings, and when they cross empty Talaat Harb Street, walking with slow, feeble steps, either propping one another up or supporting themselves on their walking sticks, they look as though they had just arisen from the dead, brushed off the grave dust, and come.

In Groppi's they sit at one table, which never changes, next to the window. There they eat breakfast, converse, and read the French newspapers until the time comes for Sunday Mass, when they set off together for church.

That morning they were all in their best get-up. The old men had shaved carefully, polished their two-tone English shoes, and put on their three-piece suits and old ties, though the latter were crumpled and crooked. They were wrapped in ancient, heavy overcoats whose colors had faded and which they removed the moment they entered the restaurant, as convention required.

The old women, those once skittish charmers, were wearing clothes that had been in fashion thirty years ago and had powdered their wrinkled faces, but the old men without exception were careful to observe the rules of etiquette, standing back to allow them to go first, helping them to remove their coats and to fold them neatly and carefully, and pulling out chairs so that they could sit down, after which they would compete at telling them curious and amusing anecdotes. Nor had the women forgotten how to let out *oohs* and *aahs* of astonishment and gentle, delicate laughs.

For these old people, the Sunday table is a moment of happiness, after which they surrender once more to their total and terrifying solitude. All they have left is likely to be a large apartment in the middle of the city, coveted by the landlord and the neighbors. The rooms are spacious, the ceilings high and the furniture ancient and neglected, with worn upholstery; the paint on the walls is peeling and the bathroom, of old-fashioned design, is in need of renovations the budget for which remains forever out of reach; and memories—and only memories—inhabit every corner, in the form of beloved black and white photographs of children (Jack, Elena) laughing charmingly, children who are now old men and mature women who have emigrated to America, speak on the telephone at Christmas, and send tasteful colored postcards, as well as monthly money orders, which the old people spend a whole day standing in long, slow lines to collect, counting the banknotes twice just to be sure once they have finally cashed them, and folding them and shoving them well down into their inside pockets.

Despite their age, their minds retain an amazing capacity to recall the past with total clarity, while inside themselves they harbor the certainty of an impending end, always accompanied by the questions, When? and How? They hope that the journey will end calmly and respectably but terrifying apprehensions of being murdered during a robbery, of a long, painful illness, or of a sudden death on the street or in a café haunt them.

That particular morning, I noticed something familiar about the face of one of the old ladies. She was sitting among the old people, her face embellished with a heavy coating of powder and on her head was a green felt hat decorated with a rose made of red cloth. I went on watching her and when I heard her voice I was sure. It must have looked strange—a staid man in his forties, rushing forward and bending over her table. I addressed her impatiently. "Tante Zitta?"

Slowly she raised her head toward me. Her eyes were old now and clouded with cataracts and the cheap glasses she wore were slightly askew, giving the impression that she was looking at something behind me. I reminded her who I was, spoke to her warmly of the old days, and asked after Antoine. She listened to me in silence with a slight, neutral smile on her old face and for so long that I thought I might have made a mistake, or that she had completely lost her wits. A moment passed and then I found her pushing herself up with her hands on the table, rising slowly until she was upright, and stretching out her arms, from which the sleeves of her dress fell back to reveal their extreme emaciation. Then Tante Zitta drew my head toward her and reached up to plant on it a kiss.